I0546111

HAWK & EAGLE

Steel Patriots MC

Book 9

Mary Kennedy

Copyright © 2020 by Mary Kennedy

All rights reserved.

This book is a work of fiction. The names, characters, places, and incidents are products of the writer's imagination or have been used fictitiously and are not to be constructed as real. Any resemblance to persons, living or dead, actual events, locales, or organizations is entirely coincidental.

No part of this book may be reproduced in any form or by any electronic or mechanical means, including information storage and retrieval systems, without written permission form the author, except for the use of brief quotations in a book review.

Contents

CHAPTER ONE

"Ryan? Why were you in another fight today, son?" asked the ever-patient, ever-loving father of Ryan and Tyran O'Neal. The seven-year-old twin boys were so identical that he often had difficulty telling them apart until they spoke. Ryan was his loud, jokester, test-the-limits son. Tyran was quieter, more thoughtful, an old man already, in a seven-year-old body.

Things had been even worse since their mother left. No notice, no indication, not even so much as a long letter. Just a simple note: *I need to start over – I'm sorry*. That really didn't help two little boys who still needed their mother's guidance every day. He was trying his best, really, he was, but Ryan was definitely testing the limits for Dillon O'Neal today.

"Son, I asked you a question. Why did you get in another fight today?" Dillon looked at Tyran, who stood like a statue next to his brother, never revealing his brother's secrets or indiscretions.

"Tommy Schneider called us bastards," he said, kicking at the dirt. Dillon nodded his head and frowned.

"I see. Do you know what that means?" he asked his son.

"Yea, we don't have parents."

"No, that's not exactly what it means. To be a bastard child means that you don't know who your father is." Ryan's head snapped up, staring at this father. "Do you know who your father is?"

"Yes, sir. You are."

"That's right, Ryan. And do you know who your mother is?"

"Yes, sir, but she left us," he said, looking down at his shoes again.

"No, son, she didn't leave you. She left me. I don't think your mother loved me anymore, but I know for a fact she loved the two of you. How could she not?" he grinned. "No woman goes through thirteen hours of labor to push out two seven-pound babies, stays up with them all night when they're sick, loves them, rocks them, and bakes for them if she doesn't love them. She loved the both of you. I just don't think she wanted to be here any longer."

"Wh-why didn't she take us with her?" asked Tyran quietly. Dillon knelt in front of his sons and gripped a big hand over each shoulder.

"Well, Ty, I think maybe she believed that young men belonged to their fathers. I know you miss her; I miss her too. Have I done something wrong? Do you need me to change something I'm doing?" he asked cautiously.

"No, Dad," said Ryan quickly. "You're the best dad in the world, really. We just... we just thought maybe we did something wrong." Dillon swallowed, turning his head slightly so that his sons wouldn't see the tears forming in his eyes.

"You two have done nothing wrong – nothing. You're the best sons a man could ask for... except the fighting," he winked at Ryan. "Fighting is a last resort, Ryan, you know that. You boys are big, bigger than most of the kids in your class, and that's an advantage. Now, when you're grown men, and you go off into the world and decide what you want to do, then you can use that size to your benefit if you feel it's necessary."

"I want to be a Marine like you, Dad," said Ryan. Tyran looked sideways at his twin, an unsettled feeling pooled in his gut, but he said nothing. He rarely said anything. Ryan did all the talking, and if their father knew the truth, the truth was Tyran did most of the fighting.

"I'd be proud to have you become a Marine, Ry, but I want you to do what you want to do. I want you to become whatever you want. You can be a lawyer or a doctor, maybe a teacher or a veterinarian. Anything you want to be. Don't limit yourself." Ty nodded his head, his dark blonde hair flopping in his eyes.

"Okay you two, wash up for dinner. We're going to the officer's club for dinner tonight. It's Colonel Jordan's retirement dinner. Put on your nice clothes and comb your hair. Ryan? You too, son, wash your face." Both boys took off inside the house, and Dillon just shook his head. Walking along the sidewalk in front of the house was Debbie Combs, a young mother of a little girl who lived three houses down.

In Dillon's head, she was the epitome of a bored military wife, looking for excitement in the form of anything in a uniform. She was a woman with too much enhancement, too much time, and not enough to occupy her days.

"Hi, Dillon," she said with a pretty smile and wave. "How are you?" She sauntered across the grass toward him, stopping just inches from his body, her fingernails crawling up his shirt.

"Debbie. I'm doing well. John still deployed?" he asked, knowing that he was.

"Of course, he's always gone. Makes a woman lonely sometimes. You know how that is, Dillon. I know you must get lonely too," she cooed.

"Honestly, Debbie, the boys keep me busy and work. I don't have time to date, and even if I did, it wouldn't be to a married woman." She grinned at him, her head tilted back, laughing. Her breasts were about to burst out of her top.

"Oh, Dillon, you are a breath of fresh air. I don't want to date you, honey," she said, leaning closer to his ear, "I want to fuck you, make you scream my name. Now, I know your dick gets hard, and I bet it's a big one. You just give me a call any time you want me to help you out. I'll be waiting."

"Thanks for the offer, Debbie, but the answer will always be no." Ty watched the exchange with his father and the neighbor lady. He felt a certain sense of pride for his father but wasn't really sure why. His brother was tossing his clothes around the room, trying to find a clean shirt.

"Why do you think Mrs. Combs keeps coming over here even though dad doesn't like her?" he asked his brother.

"Seriously, Ty? I mean, I know we're only seven, but she wants to have sex with Dad." Tyran whipped his head around at his brother.

"That's disgusting! No, she doesn't!"

"Yes, she does. You need to look at those girly magazines I have under the bed. Girls are awesome when they get older. I can't wait to touch one."

"That's gross, Ryan!" yelled his brother.

"Whatever, just get dressed, or we'll be late." Tyran dressed beside his brother, careful to not wear exactly what he was wearing, hoping that any slight color or pattern changes would let people see how different they were. Of course, it never worked. They were just too identical.

It would be ten years later when Ryan snuck in the house at two a.m., smelling like cheap perfume and sex. He'd finally figured out what everyone was talking about with Mrs. Combs, and she was more than happy to teach him all the things he needed to know. Tyran thought his brother was a sex-depraved addict, but he enjoyed hearing his stories.

When they graduated from high school, Ryan woke up one morning telling his brother to come with him to run some errands. Little did he know that one of those errands was the Marine Corps Recruitment Office. Two hours later, the papers signed, Tyran stared at his brother, incapable of understanding how he'd convinced him to join.

It would be during boot camp that he got his first shot at knowing why those girly magazines were so amazing. He'd done some heavy petting and kissing in high school, but by that time, Ryan was an experienced prick, fucking any girl who would let him, and there were a lot of them lined up.

His experience didn't seem all that memorable. The girl was the same age as him but seemed way too experienced for his tastes, and she chewed her gum the entire time. He'd felt dirty when they finished but happy that his first experience was done. He would certainly have many more, but many of them were to protect his brother.

His fucking idiot of a brother who always seemed to attract women like bar flies, wanting a piece of the big package he constantly tr ed to display. Ryan thought nothing of taking two or three or even four women back to their room, having one do his brother while the others worked him. Tyran wouldn't even consider doing it, except that his stupid brother was nearly robbed and killed by a woman who drugged him and then went through his wallet, letting her pimp boyfriend in the room to take care of the rest.

Tyran walked in to catch them and beat the shit out of the boyfriend, and scared the daylights out of the girl. When his brother woke and learned the story, he swore he would never do it again… without Tyran being there to help.

He was, by definition, his brother's keeper, and it was getting old fast.

CHAPTER TWO

"Sgts. O'Neal?" called the captain to the waiting men outside his office door. The two men stepped inside, their identical faces and bodies still making him shake his head even after a year of knowing them.

"Sir," they said in unison.

"Head over to spec op force tent and ask for Ghost. You're needed," he said without even looking at the two men. "And Sgt. R. O'Neal? Do not, under any circumstances, fuck this up. Understood?"

"Understood, sir," he said, saluting his captain and then following his brother out of the tent. They walked between the long rows of huts, saying nothing at first, and then, as always, Ryan had to break the silence.

"What the fuck was that all about? Don't fuck it up? I don't fuck shit up," he mumbled.

"Actually, you do, Ry." His brother never stopped, just kept walking toward their destination, knowing that if this was a Special Forces tent, something big was going down.

"What do I fuck up?" he yelled a little too loud.

"Let's start with the last mission," said Ty. "You were so busy watching the belly dancers you almost missed the mark."

"But I didn't, and I was watching the belly dancers to make the mark think I was distracted," he grinned.

"You were distracted. Then, of course, there was the incident in San Diego with the general's daughter. The fucking general's daughter, Ry. All the fucking women in San Diego, hot women, and you had to chase down and fuck her Not just fuck her. Noooo, you had to cart her off to wine country for four days, fuck her silly, and then leave her. You. Left. Her, Ry. Left that twenty-year-old girl in the middle of wine country alone."

"I can't help it I was called back in the middle of the night," he said, smirking at his brother.

"You think this is funny? Nothing about any of this is funny, Ryan. I'm fucking serious about this. If you want to blow your career, do it, but don't take me with you. We're attached at the fucking hip because we're twins."

"No, we're attached at the fucking hip, brother, because we're damn good at blowing off heads from a mile away. We are the best fucking snipers the Marine Corp has, and they like us working together. That's why we're attached at the fucking hip." Ryan sped up, his brother running to catch up with him.

"You know what's really shitty about all this, Ryan? I didn't even want to join the fucking Marines. I did it to protect your stupid ass because you never think to look over your shoulder. You never think of the fucking consequences. As kids, it was picking fights with three or four guys at a time. As a teenager, it was stealing girls or the best one, fucking Mrs. Combs with her husband in the next damn room!"

"That was classic," he grinned.

"Ryan! You're not fucking listening to me. You have a death wish. Great! I do not. Do not fucking blow this for us. I know about this team – Ghost. I do not want this fucked up." Ty gripped his brother's arm and yanked back. "Promise me, Ryan. Just one fucking time, do as I ask. Do what I need."

"Fine, I'm not sure why you've got a hard-on over this, but fine."

Tyran wasn't convinced his brother was going to act like a normal human being, but he would do his best to do most of the talking, and hopefully, this guy Ghost would trust them. He'd heard rumors of a mixed Special Forces team that was taking on missions no one else wanted, and he wanted to be a part of it. Maybe even part of it without his brother. He knocked on the door and heard the big booming voice.

"Come in!" Stepping through, they adjusted their eyes to the darkness of the room and saluted whoever it was in front of them.

"Sir! Sgt. Ryan O'Neal and Sgt. Tyran O'Neal reporting for duty."

"Put your hand down, sergeant," said Ghost. "Which one of you is which?"

"I'm Tyran O'Neal, sir. They call me Eagle. This is my brother Ryan O'Neal; they call him Hawk." Ghost nodded at the two young men. They couldn't be much older than nineteen or twenty.

"According to your captain, you two have more confirmed kills than the rest of the camp combined." He noticed a small smirk on the face of the one named Ryan and grimaced. He could tell what that look was. It was the look of a young man who thought he had the world by the balls.

"Something funny, Hawk?"

"Oh, no, sir, just, well, it's correct. We have more kills than anyone else in the camp."

"Yep, that's what I said. It's a fact, nothing for you to be grinning about. We have more Special Forces missions than any other spec ops team on the planet. You don't see me grinning." The smirk disappeared, and the younger man swallowed. "Hear me loud and clear, *Hawk*. This is a team. We operate and move together, and we rely on one another. If one person, one fucking egotistical jackass fucks up, the whole team suffers. I don't need divas on my team. I need team players who will follow fucking orders and get shit done. Am I clear?" The big man took a step forward, and for the first time in his life, Ryan felt small.

"Ghost asked if he was clear," said the bass voice coming from his left. A giant man, black face and eyes towering above his six-foot-two, stared down at him.

"Sorry, sir, yes, I understand. My apologies. I often use humor to cope, inappropriately, obviously." Ghost nodded but turned to confront Tyran.

"You're obviously the quiet one, but I hear stellar things about you. I'm assigning you with my group. Your brother will be with Zulu and his group. Mission details will be given as we go. Pack your gear and be ready. We leave in an hour."

The two young men saluted again and walked out of the hut saying nothing as they rushed toward their own bunks.

"Thanks for not blowing that, Ryan," said Ty.

"No problem," he mumbled. "I'm sorry if I've fucked you over somehow, Ty. That was never my intention. You're my brother, and I love you more than anything. That team? Those badass motherfuckers back there? They are the kind of men I want us associated with. I only hope we get the chance to prove it."

It would be more than a year before Ghost and his team were forced to retire, leaving Eagle and Hawk to find a new team to work with. The problem was no one was like Ghost or his band of men. They'd grown familiar, comfortable with them, and didn't want to have to work for anyone else. Until their commitment was up, they were stuck.

After five years and three days, they left the Marine Corps and the West Coast headed to Virginia to become a part of the new Ghost team – the Steel Patriots. Riding their motorcycles the almost twenty-seven hundred miles, they pulled up dirty, tired, and hungry but happy to see their teammates once more.

"Find a room, boys!" yelled Whiskey. "Let the fun begin."

New missions, new businesses, new faces, new friends, yet they still felt a part of the brotherhood. For Ryan, he had everything he wanted – brothers, booze, and pussy. For Ty, he was still stuck in the rut of watching his brother. Something had to change. He needed something. Seeing Ace find Charlie was the ultimate blow for him.

If Ace, the completely anti-social, contact-phobic geek, could find a woman like Charlie, surely there was hope for him out there. He needed to separate himself from his brother. Find his own way, and that was going to be painful.

Like a band-aid, just rip it off.

CHAPTER THREE

New Year's Eve. Another fucking year staring at my idiot brother doing stupid shit and trying to fuck anything that will spread for him, thought Eagle. His twin, Hawk, was on the other side of the big restaurant/bar flirting with three women, all a little tipsy, all a little under-dressed, and all eye-fucking him and his twin. One of them kept crooking her finger at him, trying to get him to come over and join them. He didn't even bother to acknowledge her, turning away.

"Not this shit again," he muttered.

Eagle liked sex as much as the next man, but his brother was on a whole other level. He often fucked two or three women at once, even getting his twin in on the action, not that he needed help getting action. Eagle wasn't opposed, but there were only so many times you could see your brother's dick driving into some girl and then having her want the same thing from him.

Deciding he couldn't sit and watch the show happening with his twin, he stepped outside in the frigid night air for a breather. Times like this, he wished he smoked, but then again, that's exactly what had killed their father. Emphysema was a bitch, and when you're not even sixty, it's even worse. He kicked a huge pile of snow, causing flakes and snowballs to go flying through the air.

"What did that snow ever do to you?" said the melodic voice behind him. He turned, ready to give a smart-ass response, instead seeing the most luscious creature he'd ever laid eyes on. At six-foot-two, Eagle and his brother were both tall. His nearly two hundred and ten pounds of muscle was something he prided himself in, working out every day.

This woman was probably five-feet-nine, her blunt cut, mahogany hair kissing her jaw as she moved. She had full red lips, enhanced by nothing, it seemed, other than genetics. Her eyes were huge, almost too big for her face, almost. They were the color of sea glass, green and blue combined, fringed in thick black lashes.

Tinley stared at the younger man in front of her. Oh, my goodness, said her ovaries. This was one well-built male. His dark blonde, almost brown hair was cut stylishly, his chiseled features sported a neatly trimmed beard, but it was his muscles flexing through the crew neck sweater that made her thighs clench together. Shit, he was hot – and young.

"Sorry," he said, staring at her, "did I get you?" He looked her up and down as if searching for damage, but what he was really doing was taking in the sight of this creature in front of him. She was spectacular.

"No, I'm safe from the snow monster," she said, grinning as she held out a long slender hand. "I'm Tinley."

"Eagle, ummm, Tyran or Ty, but my teammates call me Eagle," he said, suddenly feeling flushed. She smiled again, nodding up at him.

"Those snow piles can be real little shits," she grinned. "I had a fight with one yesterday trying to get my car out of the driveway. Unfortunately, the snow won, which is how I learned about this place. The car is now in that garage over there."

"Yea, hey, you wanna go inside and have a drink?" he asked.

"Oh, I'd love to, but I'm waiting on..." she looked up as a woman walked toward her. She had the same mahogany hair, only longer, same tall body, her eyes a shade closer to blue than green. "There she is. Ty, this is my daughter Keegan. Keegan, this is Ty." You could have pushed Eagle over with a feather. Her daughter?

"Hi there," she said with a huge infectious smile. "Way to go. Mom! He's hot."

"Keegan," said her mother under her breath. "I'm sorry. My daughter doesn't often find her manners or her filter." Eagle couldn't help but laugh.

"I think I know what you mean. I have a twin brother inside who is exactly like that." Keegan's eyes grew wide as she looked the man up and down.

"A twin!? Yes! Let's go, handsome. Introduce me to your brother," said Keegan, storming through the doors. Tinley bit her lower lip and shook her head.

"I'm really sorry. She's... assertive," said her mother. Eagle could not get over the fact that the woman in front of him was the mother of a girl old enough to drink. She was stunning, and his dick was definitely taking note.

"Assertive can be good. What I want to know is whether or not you'll let me buy you that drink."

"Oh, listen, you're adorable, really, handsome, sexy – shit," she mumbled, nervously nibbling on her bottom lip, "I mean, you're very good-looking, and obviously, you could have any young woman you want in that room, and I bet there are a lot of young women in that room who might like you, and I'm forty years old, and I'm sure that's a lot older than you, and I haven't been with a man in almost fifteen years, and you didn't need to hear that, and oh

damn, I'm messing this up." Eagle let a big grin slip from his sexy lips and looked down at her.

"You're not messing anything up, Tinley. Take a breath. A drink. One drink."

"Okay, one drink."

She sighed, and he wanted to inhale that sigh into his body, hear it again and again as

she lay beneath him. He lay his big palm at her lower back and guided her through the doors,

looking for a place to sit. In the far corner was a table for two, and he pushed her in that

direction. He noticed Tinley looking for her daughter and caught her on the dance floor with

Skull.

"She's there," he said, leaning down in her ear, "dancing with a friend of mine." Tinley

nodded and smiled.

"She's definitely not shy," she chuckled. "I was worried about her going out alone

tonight, so I agreed to come out for a little while."

"I'm glad you did, Tinley. You look beautiful, by the way." She flushed a bright pink,

running her hands over her straight dark hair.

"Thank you. As I so elegantly said outside," she said, rolling her eyes, "you're very

handsome, Ty, but you're also very young."

"Does that matter?" he asked, tilting his head. "I think you're beautiful, and I don't give

a shit that you're forty. Age doesn't mean anything, Tinley. I served in the Marines. I work a job where I see more shit than I should, and I know what I want." She swallowed and looked directly into his eyes.

"Wow, you're, ummm, direct, aren't you?" she said.

"Yep, life is too short not to be. That idiot at the bar is my twin brother but let me be really clear. We are nothing alike other than in appearance. He, like your daughter, has no filter. I'm also ashamed to say, most of the time, he doesn't have any morals and is typically described by our friends as a man-whore. Now, I'm not a virgin. I've had my experiences, but I am far more selective than my brother."

Tinley's eyes were wide with the young man's statement, simply staring in awe.

"Now, you are the first woman who has genuinely intrigued me on every level. I'd like to get to know you, just you and me. I suggest we start with a dance. What do you say?"

She tried to find a reason not to dance with Ty but was struggling to get there. He was not the kind of man who would typically approach her. He was so gorgeous he could be on the cover of a fitness magazine. She had stretch marks and scars.

New Year, Tinley. New Year, new you.

"Okay, we start with a dance," she said, blushing again.

"You look fucking beautiful when you do that," he grinned.

"Do what?"

"Blush. It's this gorgeous pink hue that goes beautifully with your hair." He placed that big hand at her lower back once again, his long fingers stretching just enough that the fingertips brushed the top of her ass cheeks. He smelled like whiskey and cinnamon. His big hand

enveloped hers, and she swallowed at the sight of his long, thick fingers.

"You obviously work out a lot," she said, smiling up at him. He nodded.

"Yep. Part of the job and a carryover of my time in the Marines. Steep Patriots, we own

this club, as well as the garage and gym out front and the clinic down the road. I help with the

gym and the garage, but we also take on special assignments."

"I see, so my car is in your garage?" she asked, smiling.

"It is, beautiful, and I promise I'll make sure it's taken care of." She smiled up at him,

and something about that smile made him swell with pride. "What about you, sweet Tinley?

What do you do for a living?"

"Nothing quite so exciting. I'm an accountant at a local firm here in the valley."

"Are you from this area?" he asked. She shook her head, biting her lower lip and

looking away for a moment.

"No, no. I-I moved here when Keegan was seven."

"You divorced?" he asked. Tinley stopped the dance and tried to take a step backwards,

but Ty wouldn't let her, holding her against his body. "You don't have to answer, sweet girl. I

was just curious."

"I-I'm sorry. I wasn't married, but it wasn't a good situation. I had Keegan at eighteen

and tried to make the relationship work. It just, it wasn't a good place for me. I was finally able

to get away when she was seven. We-we lived in the Las Vegas area before coming here." He just nodded, and Tinley bit that lip again. Ty didn't like the sound of that. "Finally able to get away" meant that something or someone was holding her there.

"I-I can't believe I told you that. I've never told anyone that," she whispered.

"Glad you did, beautiful," he smiled down at her. "Doesn't matter to me at all. I like you, Tinley. So far, I like everything about you, and I don't want this to just be a New Year's Eve dance."

"Man, you really know how to sweep a woman off her feet. Just how old are you, Ty?" she asked with trepidation.

"Twenty-seven, beautiful Tinley."

"Twenty... seven..." she whispered. "I barely remember that."

He laughed a deep rumbling sound, his chest vibrating against her own, and she became painfully aware of the fact that she wasn't wearing a bra. Keegan convinced her to wear one of her dresses, the spaghetti straps and backless feature not allowing for a bra. As his chest rumbled against her own, her nipples took notice.

Thankfully, they were mostly concealed by the shimmering, sequined fabric, but his hand immediately found her bare back and pressed her closer as a slow song came on.

"Your skin feels like silk, honey," he whispered in her ear.

"Ty, I... no man has ever said things like that to me."

"Then you're dating the wrong men. In fact, scratch that. I'd like to ask you here and now to not date any other men, just me."

"J-just you? We just met!" she squealed a little too loudly. Ty laughed at her, leaning forward and kissing the tip of her nose.

"Yes, we did, but I'd sure like the chance to date you. Just you, Tinley. Just you, and just me. See, I think when two people are meant to be together, nothing else matters. That couple over there, the big black guy with the woman with white hair and fabulous eyes? That's my teammate Zulu and his wife, Gabrielle. They couldn't be more different if they tried. And over there, the guy with the woman on his knee? That's Ace and his fiancée, Charlie. She's three years older than him."

"Three years, Ty. Three years, not thirteen!"

"Thing is, honey, you don't look your age at all, and that's fucking hot to me. Besides the fact that you know how to hold a conversation. You haven't giggled once. I hate fucking giggling. You aren't wearing too much make-up. You seem to have your head on straight. Plus, mad respect for raising a daughter on your own and getting a degree in accounting. Fucking impressive, Tinley."

"I don't even know what to say to all that. You move so fast, I can't even keep up," she said. "I'm so flattered, Ty. You have no idea. I vomited my history on you outside." She cringed, and he laughed at her.

"I'm sorry about that. I haven't had a date since we moved here. I've been... scared to, I guess. I don't know. I'm really nervous about this. I mean, you're not just young. You look like, well, like that!" she said, waving up and down his body.

"Clarify, honey," he said, pulling her to him again.

"Ty, surely you know you're built like a damn Greek god. You're stunning. Your body, your face, your voice, damn, that voice does things to me…" She blushed again, looking away.

"What sort of things?" he whispered in her ear. Tinley swallowed and shook her head.

"I think I need a drink," she said. Ty smiled at her, nodding.

"Then let's get my girl a drink and some food. I want you to have a good time tonight, Tinley, but I want my girl sober when I make love to her for the first time, and trust me, baby, I'm going to make love to you tonight." He walked toward the bar to order their drinks and then gathered two plates of food, his brother standing beside him, chatting with a big smile on his face. He looked back toward Tinley and smiled, murmuring to herself.

"Holy fucking shit. I am in big trouble."

CHAPTER FOUR

Hawk had a woman under each arm and one standing in front of him, sliding her hand up and down his semi-hard cock. For some reason, tonight, the three blondes were not doing it for him. His brother had left him high and dry, walking outside several minutes before. Now one of the blondes, Amber... Bambi... no, Valerie... close, was trying to get him to take them to the back rooms.

"Come on, baby, you know we can make you feel good, we always do? Where's that stud brother of yours?" she asked. Ryan let a grin slip, looking down at her.

"What's the matter? I'm not enough for you anymore."

"Oh, honey, you and that big cock are always enough for us. We want to play tonight, Ryan. Come on, baby. Take us to the back. I'll fuck you while you eat out Cheri. We'll take turns like always; it will be fun." Something about tonight was really nagging at him. It just wasn't feeling right.

Could he honestly be growing a conscience? Was he finally, at twenty-seven years old, growing up? Shit, please don't let that happen. Yet nothing was right. Staring at the door, waiting for his brother to return, a tall, long-legged vision walked in. Her long mahogany hair was shiny and thick, hanging in waves down her back; he could see she had blue eyes from across the room, and that dress showed off every fucking curve.

She was stunning. And she was the exact opposite of every woman he'd ever gone for. She wasn't blonde. She wasn't filled with silicone from what he could see, and she had the unmistakable look of intelligence on her face. Looking around the room, she caught his eye and stared straight at him, at first smiling and then with a frown.

Stepping toward the bar, she set her small clutch on the surface and asked for a glass of wine. He pushed the three women aside and started to make his way down the bar.

"Hey! What the hell?" yelled Valerie. "I thought we were going to the back."

"No thanks," he said, removing her hand from his arm. "Not interested." He moved closer to the woman and ordered a beer. Turning slightly, he gave her his best smile, but she didn't even look his way. Frowning, he decided a little nudge might help. The wine in her glass jostled, and she gave him a dirty look, moving it slightly out of his reach.

"What's a beautiful thing like you doing all alone?"

"Not alone," she said, sipping her wine. "Neither are you if the three bimbos at the end of the bar are any indication. Time for you to go back to your toys, little boy." Ryan stepped back, eyes wide, staring at the young woman.

"Little boy? Baby, all you have to do is take a walk with me, and I'll show you I'm no little boy," he grinned.

"Your dick size proves nothing. I can already tell exactly what you are," she smiled.

"Oh yea," he huffed. "What is that?"

"You are a little boy with mommy issues and a complex about women. You fuck every woman you can get your hands on and leave them before they leave you. You treat them like your own personal toys, your disposable dolls. You think giving them a little of your fascinating dick will make their year. Well, news flash, asshole, they're using you, not the other way around. They're getting their fun in, fucking the good ole' boy with the decent dick, getting their freak on, and then going back to wherever they live, to their husbands and boyfriends, or in Valerie's case... girlfriends."

Ryan whipped his head around to see Valerie deep-throating one of her girlfriends. Fuck!

"So, you see, Mr. tall, dark, and has a penis, you're nothing special, not to them. I don't need another asshole in my life. I don't need another dick who comes with promises and leaves with little pieces of my soul. So, if you'll excuse me, I think I'll find a dance partner."

Ryan couldn't even form a sentence as she walked away, headed toward Skull. Placing a hand on his shoulder, the man turned and grinned down at the pretty woman, nodding. Together on the dance floor, all he could see was the flexing of her calf muscles, and those long as shit legs leading to what he was sure would be heaven.

A few minutes later, drowning in his pity, he spotted his twin brother coming in the door with another gorgeous woman looking eerily similar. Sisters? Either way, he was happy Ty was at least finally having a good time. He didn't need to spoil it with his funk, so instead, he walked over to the other single guys, sitting and bullshitting. When he noticed Tyran grabbing drinks and food, he stood to chat with him.

"Who's the fox?" he smiled.

"Don't fuck with her, Ryan. I mean it. She's fucking amazing, and I want that woman... like she's the one." His brother started to laugh and thought it probably wasn't a good idea.

"Like 'the' one," he said with air quotes.

"Yep. She's fucking beautiful." Tyran looked around the room and nodded toward the dance floor. "That's her daughter."

"What?!" he said a little too loudly. "What the fuck, Ty?"

"I know. She's a good bit older, but, brother, there is nothing old about that woman. The daughter is more your type," he grinned.

"Yea, I don't think so. She's got a viper tongue and badger temper. I don't need a bitch like that in my life." His brother looked at him and nodded.

"Don't you?" Ty walked back to his table with two plates full of food and two drinks. He sat down, pulled Tinley closer, and something inside Ryan broke a little. His brother looked happy. For the first time in his life, he looked fucking happy... without him.

"Shit, maybe I do have mommy issues."

CHAPTER FIVE

Tinley had never danced so much in her entire life, and Ty was a great dancer. Who would have believed, with all those muscles, he'd be able to move like that! She kept pinching herself to see if it was real. He was handsome, had a great body, was intelligent, served his country, and as hard as she tried, she could not find one damn thing wrong with him other than his age.

As midnight neared and the party favors were handed out, he pulled her with him to the center of the dance floor for the countdown.

"To us, Tinley," he said, raising the glass of champagne. "To our new year."

"To us," she whispered as he dropped his lips to hers. Ty gripped her waist and pressed her against his growing erection. Tinley could barely breathe she was so hot for this man. She'd been careful not to drink too much, knowing it might send her over the edge. As the countdown started, their kiss never broke, and Ty's rigid cock poked into her belly.

She'd never wanted a man like she did this one. There was something about him that made everything in her body tingle. Of course, the only man she'd ever had was Keegan's father, and that was a disaster. No, this man was different.

"... three, two, one... happy new year, honey," he said against her lips.

"Happy New Year, Ty," she said, kissing him again. She felt a tap on her shoulder and turned.

"Hey, Mom… and friend," she grinned, "I'm going to stay here tonight with my new friend, Skull."

"Skull?" said Tinley, raising an eyebrow.

"Hi," said the handsome young man standing next to her daughter, "I'm Scott Crawford, but my team name is Skull. I promise, I'm a good guy."

"He is, Tinley," said Ty, smiling down at her. "I'd trust him with my life, and, in fact, have on more than one occasion. He's a good man." Tinley nodded.

"I'm sorry, I didn't mean to question you. Keegan is twenty-two. She can do whatever she likes. I'm just a worrying mom."

"Well, if you don't mind me saying so, you look more like her sister than her mom. Great genes," said Skull, smiling.

"That's what I've been telling her," said Ty, kissing her temple. Keegan smiled at her mom and winked.

"If I may, Tinley, let me tell you that there's not another man in here better than Ty. He's solid. I've known the man for almost seven years now, and he's never once told me anything but truth. Don't get hung up on age," he said with a wink. Skull waved as he pulled Keegan toward the big steel door. As they passed Ryan, he frowned at his friend, watching as the gorgeous woman tagged behind him.

"Your brother doesn't look happy," she said, nodding toward him.

"Yea, well, I think my brother was an asshole to Keegan. If my instincts are right, and they usually are, he tried to pick her up, and she put him in his place." Tinley laughed and nodded.

"That sounds like my daughter. She's not afraid to say whatever is on her mind. She's a bit of a free spirit. I don't judge. She's a young woman who wants to experience what life has to offer. I know that she's smart, practices safe sex, and chooses her partners carefully. That's all a mom can ask for."

"I think that's pretty amazing that you feel that way. She seems like a nice girl," he said, smiling. Tinley laughed, shaking her head. "What?"

"You said a nice 'girl' like she's a decade younger than you. She's only five years younger than you, Ty."

"Is that what's bothering you? That your daughter is closer to my age than you are?"

"I-I don't know. Maybe, no, yes," she bit her lip, turning away, but Ty gripped her chin, pulling her back to look at him.

"Listen to me, Tinley, last time, baby. I don't give a fuck what your age is. It does not matter to me at all. I like you, fucking think you're amazing, and want to give this a chance, but if you don't, please don't start something that might break me. Because I think for the first time in my life, Tinley, you are a woman that could break me."

Holy hell, this man, this man was going to break down every defense she so carefully constructed these last fifteen years. Fifteen years of quiet dates for coffee or lunch, never dinner. Dinner might lead to something she wasn't ready for, and now, in less than three hours, this man had her thinking all sorts of infinite possibilities.

"What will it be, Tinley? Will you give us a chance?" She swallowed hard, looking down at the four-inch heels that were suddenly killing her feet.

"Y-yes, I'd like to try, but-but promise, Ty, promise me that if you at any time feel like you can't do this, that you'll tell me." He shook his head, pulling her closer, almost wrapping her in his own skin.

"I will not change my mind, baby. Will you come with me to my rooms upstairs?"

"You live here? In the bar?" she asked. Ty laughed at her, gripping her hand.

"Come on, baby, let me show you. It's not what you think." She followed behind him, his long legs difficult to keep up with. He pressed a palm to a flat screen on the door, and the big steel door opened, then quickly shut behind them. Down a hallway, there was another steel door with the same security. He opened it, holding it for her as they stepped through.

The wood floors were polished to a meticulous shine, pictures of custom-made cars and motorcycles lined the walls, interspersed with photographs of people she recognized from their evening together. A long staircase led to the second floor, and Ty led her down and to the left, opening the door.

"Oh, wow, this is beautiful. I mean, it's like a luxury hotel suite," she said. Ty nodded, smiling at her. He was a meticulous house cleaner, everything in its place, which is why he and Ryan didn't share quarters. His brother was a slob!

"Yea, Ghost, he's our team lead and head of the Steel Patriots. He wanted us all to feel like we had family, that we were still part of the brotherhood we had when we were enlisted. Every man either has a home on the property or a suite like this. I have a living space, small efficiency kitchen, big bathroom, and, of course, the bed." Tinley felt herself go red once again and nodded.

"I-I'm nervous, Ty. I know you said it didn't matter, but I've had a child. I have stretch marks, and things aren't as firm as they once were." Ty pulled his shirt over his head, and Tinley's breath caught in her chest. She thought he was beautiful dressed; he was simply stunning without a shirt.

"Look at me, Tinley. Scars everywhere. Bullet here, here, and here. Knife wounds here and here. Shrapnel here and here. This scar over my eye, my asshole brother," he grinned. "We all have scars, baby." Tinley nodded again and set her clutch down on the nightstand. She kicked off her heels and then took four giant steps toward Ty, now suddenly almost six inches taller than she was.

Sliding the straps of her dress over her shoulders, she let it gently slide down her body, puddling at her feet. All that was left was Tinley in a tiny scrap of cloth. Her glorious body standing before him to behold.

"Fucking hell, Tinley. You're stunning, precious girl, fucking stunning. Take off the panties, baby," he said, swallowing hard. Tinley nodded and then shook her head. Walking one step closer, she unhooked his belt buckle and then unzipped his trousers.

Ty kicked off his shoes, letting the pants fall as he stepped out of them. Tinley's tiny fingers slid beneath his waistband and shoved the boxer briefs down, his thick cock bouncing toward her. Her eyes grew wide, and she took a half a step back.

"I'm not sure… I don't think…"

"I promise, precious girl, it will fit. You're made for me, Tinley; I just know it, honey." She wiggled out of the lace thong, the crotch already soaked with her desire. Ty just stood for a few minutes staring at her, taking her in, her beautiful, perfect breasts, the tiniest curve of her belly, the slight swell of her hips. She was fucking gorgeous.

"I-I need you, Ty," she whispered. That was all he needed to hear. Grabbing her by the waist, he pulled her to him, wrapping her long legs around him, his tip feeling the heat from her center.

"Fuck, Tinley, baby, I need you now. I don't think I'll last the first time, honey."

"Now," she said, kissing her, sliding her tongue inside his mouth. "Now, worry about slow later." He nodded, laying her on his bed. Reaching into his nightstand, he grabbed the condom and slid it along his thick, long cock as Tinley watched, her eyes never leaving his fingers. That gaze made Ty want to explode all over her.

"Open, baby," he said against her lips. "Fuck, woman, you are so fucking beautiful. Oh shit, Tinley, you're soaked for me, aren't you, baby?"

"Y-yes, you make me want you. I need you," she said breathlessly. Ty touched his big head to her opening, stretching her as he started to slide through, his big dick pushing a little at a time. When he couldn't stand it anymore, he drove home, hitting the very depths of Tinley.

"Damn, baby, that is one tight pussy, honey…"

"Fif-fifteen years, Ty. I told you," she said, moaning against his lips. Tinley rolled her hips into his big pelvis, feeling the length of him rubbing in all the right spots, the perfect spots that no other man had ever touched. "Oh, wow, that's-that's perfect…"

"Fuck yea, it's perfect, baby. I knew it, honey; I just knew it." His mouth captured hers as he ground his body into her own, their skin slapping against each other. "Baby, I'm so close…"

"Uhhh," she cried out, releasing her own orgasm, which was perfect for Ty as he pumped three times and spilled inside the condom. Slowing, he kissed her and stood to tie off the condom and dispose of it. Settling beside her again, he ran his big, callused hands up and down her body, gliding down to the glistening thatch of dark hair in a long slender strip.

"Fuck, woman, you're beautiful," he growled. Tinley reached up a hand. Gripping his hair, she pulled him toward her, tasting him again.

"You're the one who is beautiful, Ty. I've never seen a man built like you. Your, well, your dick is nothing short of amazing," she said, grinning. Ty chuckled, kissing one perfect nipple and then the other.

"Oh, baby, you are something else. Stay with me tonight, Tinley. Don't leave, honey, stay and let's enjoy New Year's Day together. My friends will be having a big dinner."

"I don't know, Ty. Won't that be awkward? I mean, I'm just some random woman you brought home."

"Tinley, I've told you, baby. I don't bring random women home. Listen, honey, no one, and I mean no one, gets through that second steel door to our private quarters unless they mean something to us, something special."

"Wh-where is Keegan?" she asked, suddenly concerned. Ty smiled at her.

"Seems your daughter is smarter than you think. Skull sent me a text. He put her in a guest room. They didn't sleep together."

"Oh," she said quietly. That was a surprise. Skull was exactly the kind of man Keegan would usually go for. "So, we would have breakfast with your friends?"

"That's usually the practice around here when we wake up," he grinned, sliding a finger down between those perfect folds.

"Ohh, mmm, ummm, right. Okay, wow, I can't think when you do that," she whispered.

"That's the goal, beautiful. Say you'll stay, honey," he said, pulling on a big nipple.

"Oh, wow, yes, yes, I'll stay," she said, pulling his mouth down to hers. "If-if you let me do something."

"Precious girl, I'll let you do anything. What?" Tinley pushed him to his back and straddled his thighs. His eyes got big as her breasts fell against her chest, her hair tucked behind her ears.

"I want to suck you. I mean, I want to try. I've never..."

"Sweetheart, there is nothing you can't do to my body. Do whatever you want to do, Tinley, anything." She nodded, bending down, her dark hair tickling his thighs. That perfect mouth opened, and she held him firmly against her lips, then, with a flick of her tongue, took him inside the warm, wet hole.

Ty's groans of pleasure were all the encouragement she needed, her tongue swirling around him, tasting him on her tongue. He was salty and warm, masculine, but something about him was sweet, his velvety skin so in contrast to the roughness of the man. All she knew was that she wanted to taste all of him. His hips jerked against her, and she knew he was getting close. Reaching down, she massaged his full, heavy balls, and he groaned.

"Tin... baby..." She nodded up at him and pressed forward, releasing his entire load in that pretty mouth. Tinley felt it hit her throat and swallowed, loving the taste of him on her tongue, in her mouth. Sitting up, she smiled at him, wiping her lips with one long finger. Ty gripped her shoulders and flattened her to the bed. "Fair is fair, baby girl."

His mouth was like a divining rod, hunting for her taste. The tongue flicked her hard clit, his fingers and tongue in and out of her folds, licking her juices. She gripped his hair, pushing him harder into her, fucking his whisker-covered face, the roughness against her skin erotic.

"Ty... now..." she cried as his tongue moved faster, and she exploded on his lips. He gently licked her clean, like a cat licking the cream from a bowl, and then slid up between her legs, kissing her.

"I love the way you taste, baby girl," he said, smiling down at her.

"Well, surprise, surprise, Ty. I love the way you taste too. And a bigger surprise? I love the way I taste on your lips." She looked down to see him hard again and smiled. "Is that for me?"

"Beautiful, this is all for you for as long as you want it." She nodded, smiling.

"I think I'll take it... for as long as we both want it," she grinned.

"Fuck yea, that's my girl," he growled, driving into her, wrapping her legs around his body, his big balls slapping against her wet pussy. It would be three orgasms later before Ty realized he hadn't used another condom.

"Baby, don't panic, but I didn't use a condom those last few times."

"Oh, well, I'm clean," she said.

"I am too, baby. I get tested regularly. Always use a condom, but couldn't control myself with you, needed to feel you. Not worried about that, honey. What if you get pregnant? You okay with that?" he asked sincerely.

"P-pregnant? Ty, no, no, that's not okay. You don't want to have a baby with me!"

"Fuck I don't," he growled against her belly. "I can't think of anything more perfect than having my baby in your big round belly."

"Ty, we just met!"

"Doesn't matter, baby, thought I made that clear. If you're pregnant, I'll be happy as fuck. Are you telling me you're not on birth control?" Hope rose in his chest, and for the first time in his life, he was thrilled he forgot a condom.

"N-no, I-I had several miscarriages after Keegan. The doctors weren't sure I could ever carry again, but there were... extenuating circumstances." He nodded, not wanting to pry into that just yet.

"Okay, so listen to me. I want to feel you, Tinley. I want to feel that fucking perfect, beautiful, hot wet pussy wrapped around my dick, strangling me every fucking day. I don't want to wear a condom, but I will if you insist. I don't want you on birth control, but it's your body. It won't change the way I feel about you, baby."

Tinley leaned against the headboard, her naked body bared for him as he knelt in front her, resting on his heels. She pushed back her hair and let out a long slow breath.

"You floor me," she whispered. "I keep thinking this is going to be some joke."

"No joke to me, precious girl. You're mine, Tinley. I know it in my soul that you're mine. You may need some time to catch up, but that's just the way it is." She nodded in his direction, smiling.

"I think you really believe that," she said quietly.

"Truth is easy to believe, honey." Could he be for real? Was this her chance for happiness, finally after seven years of hell and fifteen years of solitude? This beautiful, magnificent specimen of a man in front of her, was he really hers?

"Okay, Ty, no birth control, no condoms. Let me just lay a few ground rules, though. I won't tolerate lying, cheating, or-or hitting," she said, staring at him. Ty flinched at that comment and made a mental note to come back to that one as well.

"Don't lie, ever. Never cheated ever, and fuck all would never cheat on you. And, I have never, in my entire life, laid a hand on a woman. I've fought my fair share of men, but never, baby, look at me, never struck a woman and would never. Clear?"

"Clear," she whispered. "Ty?"

"Yea, sweetheart," he said, sitting beside her, pulling her into his arms as he pulled the covers up over their bodies.

"I think I'm falling for you." Ty smiled and kissed her forehead.

"Good fucking thing because I've already fallen."

CHAPTER SIX

"Thank you for this, Scott," said Keegan as the man led her into a spare room. "I promise I didn't mean to lead you on. I just don't fee comfortable…" He held up a hand and shook his head.

"No explanation needed, Keegan. I'm not the kind of man who forces himself onto a woman. You're beautiful and sexy as shit, but if you're not feelin' it, honey, then this is where it ends. I had a great time with you tonight. You'll be safe here. No one can get in. The room is equipped with towels, the beds are made with fresh linens. Breakfast is usually ready by around eight on a holiday. Feel free to come down whenever, or I'll come get you."

"Thank you, Scott, really. You're a great guy." He nodded, smiling at her. Yep, that's me, a great guy with a boner that would knock down doors.

Keegan closed the door and then remembered that she wasn't sure where her mom had gotten off to. Opening the door, a familiar face came down the hall.

"Oh, it's you," she said, smirking.

"What's the matter? Skull fire early?" he laughed.

"You're such a dick, you know that? For your information, he was a gentleman. I didn't sleep with him. He was nice enough to give me a room because I think my mom is with your brother."

"Oh," he said sheepishly, "sorry about that." He felt ike a complete dick. "Really, I'm sorry. Can we please start again?" She nodded.

"I'm Ryan O'Neal. My friends call me Hawk, but that's a leftover from my time in the Marines. I work here with the Steel Patriots, and, as you know, so does my twin brother. I'm twenty-seven years old. I'm not married, no children, and I really, truly would like to get to know you better." Keegan nodded, grinning at the man.

"Nice to meet you, Ryan. I'm Keegan Oakley. My mother, as you're well aware, is in a room somewhere with your brother." She stopped, biting her lip. "Is that weird?"

"Not unless we make it weird," he laughed. "Go on, beautiful."

"Right, I'm twenty-two. I'm not married, not dating anyone, no children. I own my own hair salon in the valley. My mom is my accountant, and she's badass." Ryan laughed at that.

"You really love your mom," he said casually. She nodded, sliding down the side of the wall to sit as he did the same across from her.

"She is amazing. She had me at eighteen, and it wasn't a great situation. My dad was, well, not nice, and he didn't really want a kid; they never married. My mom put up with a lot of shit to protect me and then finally got us out of the situation when I was seven. She worked two jobs making sure I had everything I wanted until she made partner at the accounting firm.

"I mean, you saw her. She's beautiful, and the thing is, she doesn't even know it. Everyone thinks we're sisters. She has that flawless skin, an elegance when she walks. She's stunning, and she's oblivious to it."

"My brother isn't," he said, smiling at her. "Listen, as much of a piece of shit as you may think I am, my brother is the complete opposite. Ty has never wanted to bring a woman back to his rooms. He's serious about your mom." Keegan nodded, biting her full lower lip, and Hawk definitely noticed, or at least his dick did.

"She's a good bit older than him. I know it won't matter to your brother, but Mom's pretty old-fashioned about some things."

"Well, I'm not going to interfere. I saw the look on my brother's face, and I know what that means. He's happy, and it only took him a few hours to figure it out," he laughed. She nodded, staring at him. "You know, you weren't far off about me."

"Hey, listen, I'm sorry. I was being a real bitch," she said.

"No, well, maybe," he grinned, "but you were right. My mom left us when we were six. I always saw women as the enemy after that, and I suppose the way I treated them was a bit like enemies. What you said, though, about them using me? That's the first time anyone ever said those words to me, and I realized you were right."

"I'm sorry," she whispered.

"Don't be. Listen, it's going to sound cocky, but I'm good in bed. I know I am. Fuck, I've had enough practice," he groaned, shoving a hand through his hair. "I just never figured any woman would stick around. I knew they would leave me, so I left them first." She nodded and stood.

"Maybe give one a chance to stick around, Ryan," she stepped forward, and he held his breath. She placed a chaste kiss on his cheek and moved back toward her door. "Goodnight, Ryan, and if you come by the shop, I'll give that hair a good trim. It needs it."

She was smiling as she went inside, and Ryan stood in the hallway for a good fifteen minutes, grinning at the door. His cock was hard as a rock, and for the first time in his miserable life, he wasn't thinking about finding someone to stick it in. All he was thinking about was going to sleep so he could wake and have breakfast with a certain blue-eyed brunette.

CHAPTER SEVEN

As expected, the buzz at the breakfast table was around the two new women in the group. Grace introduced the women to all the wives and welcomed them as she did everyone. When they found out Keegan was a hair stylist, the girls were all making appointments with the young woman.

"Gabrielle," said Keegan.

"Gabi, honey. Just call me Gabi."

"Gabi, your hair color is spectacular. I have clients who would pay a fortune for that color and are always disappointed when I tell them they can't get from chestnut to silver in one sitting." Gabi laughed, nodding at the younger woman.

"Believe me, I hear that all the time. Or they want to know which Halloween shop I got my contact lenses," she smiled.

"That seems rude," said Tinley.

"I'm used to it," said Gabi. As the women continued to chat, Ryan looked at his brother and nudged him.

"She's beautiful, man."

"She is fucking it, brother. I have never in my life met a woman like her. It's gonna take me some convincing, but I'm gonna marry her, Ryan." His brother smiled, nodding at him.

"Listen, I had a long chat with Keegan last night, apologized. She didn't stay with Skull; she was in one of the guest rooms." Ty nodded. "I-I like her, Ty. I mean, I really like her." Ty turned to his brother, frowning. Oh shit, his man-whore brother was going to fuck this up for him.

"I know what you're thinking," he said, looking down at his plate, "we didn't do anything. That's the thing; we talked. Like for an hour, we just talked. I really like her. She called me out on my bullshit, and I have to say it was hot as fuck that she did. I know this is all weird, but I just want you to know I'm going to get to know her... the right way."

Ty watched his brother as his gaze flicked to Keegan, her pretty smiling face so much like her mother's, those long mahogany locks falling down her back. She'd borrowed some clothes from the women today and was dressed in jeans and a sweater, looking beautiful. Her mother was dressed similarly, and it was her body that had Ty firing on all cylinders.

"Be careful is all I ask, Ry. If you get to the point where you know she's not it, just please do the right thing," he asked.

"I promise, Ty. I give you my word." He nodded at his brother, watching as Tinley held Wade on her lap, making cute little noises as she fed him. His groin flooded with warmth, his heart racing as he watched her. She was fucking stunning, and, with a baby in her arms, he was losing his shit. Turning, she looked at George.

"Mister George, is there anything I can do to help with dinner?" she asked.

"Oh, now see, that's how you talk to your elders... Mister George," he said, patting her cheek. Tinley blushed. "No mister here, honey, just George, and no, nothin' for anybody to do 'cept eat when it's time."

"She's thoughtful," said Ry to his brother. "Hey, last night Keegan said something about her dad being a real piece of shit, that her mom had to run from him. What's that all about?" Ty's face darkened, and he shook his head.

"Not sure yet, but she mentioned something similar to me. Don't want to pressure her just yet. She seems skittish already. I'll figure it out, though." Keegan watched Skull and the little girl, Calla, whispering to each other in the corner and smiled. He really was a sweetheart, and she would have to figure out a friend for him because he was worth keeping. He jumped up, holding the little girl's hand, and made an announcement.

"Okay, everyone, snowman competition! Me and Calla against all of you," he said, gripping her little hand.

"You're goin' down," she said with a sneer on her face.

"Oh, you're on!" said Ryan. "Let's go, Keegan. You and me a team. What do you say?"

"Sure!" she said, jumping to her feet. "Mom? You and Ty?" Tinley looked at Ty, and he nodded.

"Absolutely, but you know I'm an expert at this," she said to her daughter. The entire room cheered as the couples filed out, all daring to beat the others.

They were thirty minutes into it when they realized there wasn't enough snow for ten snowmen, so instead pooled their efforts creating a giant snowman, but giving Calla and Scott all the credit. The little girl cheered, pumping her fist in the air as he rode her around on his shoulders.

By late afternoon, the football games were loud in the restaurant, but it was closed to regular patrons. The new year's dinner was set up buffet style, and everyone made their platters, scattering. Tinley watched with fascination as Ryan and Keegan sat on the floor across from one another. He didn't try to touch her, and her daughter wasn't throwing herself at him.

"You okay, baby?" asked Ty, kissing her cheek.

"Perfect, Ty. I can't tell you when I've had a better time anywhere. I love your friends, and I love this place. It feels… safe." He frowned, looking at her.

"Do you feel unsafe, baby?"

"N-no. I-I suppose I should tell you this. Keegan's father, he was part of a motorcycle club, although it felt more like a gang. I didn't know that when we were dating. I mean, I knew he rode but nothing else. The first time he took me to their club, well, I can tell you it was eye-opening."

"I'm sure," he said, shaking his head.

"Women were naked everywhere, giving blowjobs to men, having sex on the pool tables. I wanted to leave, but he said it would be rude. He said it was just a wild party, nothing to worry about. I was so scared. The next thing I knew, I was naked in his bed. I'm pretty sure he slipped me something in my drink, but I couldn't prove it."

"Piece of shit," growled Ty. Tinley nodded.

"Yes, he was that. When I found out I was pregnant, he claimed it wasn't his, refused to give me any help at all. My folks kicked me out, and I lived with my grandmother until Keegan was born."

"What happened after she was born?" he asked.

"He came back." She was silent for several minutes and then started to speak again. "He dragged me back to that clubhouse, told me I'd have to do something to earn my keep. I told him I didn't want to be there. I wanted to go back to my grandmother's, but he wouldn't let me. I refused to be a club whore, so I chose to cook and clean the rooms. When their president figured out that I was good with numbers, he asked me to do their bookkeeping."

"What happened, baby?" he asked, rubbing her back.

"The books were cooked. He was stealing from his own club, besides the fact that he was running illegal gambling, hookers, just about everything. I was terrified."

"What's his name, Keegan's father?" A tear slid down her cheek, and she looked away for a moment and then back toward him.

"Brick, that was his road name. He liked to hit his victims with a brick. His real name was Ralph Tolbert. The club, the club, is the Desert Bastards." Ty let out a slow whistle.

"Honey, they're fucking bad news. Every good club knows to stay away from them. They don't just run hookers, honey. They're traffickers, drug dealers. Those assholes don't do anything legal." She nodded.

"I know. It's how I knew I had to get Keegan out of there. One of the ole' ladies, her ole' man was killed in a drug raid. She was all alone and sort of adopted Keegan and me. She... saw him hit me... I was pregnant, twice, and he hit me to make sure I lost the babies." Ty pulled her to him, burying her face in his chest.

"I'm so fucking sorry, baby girl, so fucking sorry. He won't touch you again, honey, not ever. I won't let him."

"H-he doesn't know where we are. We changed our names and moved across country. I did everything I could to stay out of the news. No social media, no professional profile, nothing. Even when I was made partner at the firm, I told them I wouldn't take a photo. Keegan, she remembers the things her father did to me. When she tried to stop him, he threw her against the wall, then, then he cut off all her hair. Told her that one day she'd make a good addition to their stables."

"Oh fuuuuckkk," growled Ty. He looked at his brother, laughing with Keegan, and felt a pit grow in his stomach. With that twin connection, his brother looked up and knew immediately what to do. Asking Keegan to stand, he walked toward the back of the barn.

"I knew I had to leave, Ty. I packed everything up, took my old car to my grandmother's, and she gave me hers. I sold it in Omaha, bought another one, and then did the same in Nashville. By the time I got here, I barely had enough money for a room. Fortunately, the motel needed a bookkeeper. I worked nights so I could be with Keegan during the day, and then when I found a full-time job, enrolled in night school. I got my degree and then went to work for the firm."

"You're fucking amazing, baby girl," he said, kissing her.

"No, I ran."

"You survived, honey. That's what you're supposed to do, survive. Not just you, but you kept that beautiful daughter of yours alive too. That's incredible, babe." She nodded. "Tinley, I know you may not like this, but I feel like I need to tell Ghost about your connection to the Desert Bastards. We don't want that kind of shit coming this way, but if it does, we'll be prepared for it."

"M-maybe I should go," she whispered.

"Nope. Not fucking happening, Tinley. I told you, honey, you're mine. All I'm saying is we don't like surprises, so I think we should tell him."

She nodded, curling into his big strong body, breathing in the scent of his cologne and the pine from outside.

"I don't know how I lived without you, Ty, and that scares the shit out of me."

"I know, baby. Believe me, I know. But here's the thing, you won't ever have to live without me again. This is it, Tinley. You and me, baby, this is it." She looked up at him with those beautiful blue-green eyes and smiled.

"I believe you, Ty. I believe you."

CHAPTER EIGHT

"Hey, what's wrong?" asked Keegan as Ryan led her down the long hallway. "Ryan? You're scaring me. Where are you taking me?"

"Damn," he said, stopping in the hallway, "I didn't mean to scare you, Keegan. I want to talk to you... alone. Can we do that?" She looked at him and noted the serious expression, and nodded. Ryan opened the door to his room, and then thought better of it, the mess and stench of male sweat almost overwhelming to him.

"Can we sit in your room?" he asked. She nodded, opened the door, and sat on the edge of the loveseat.

"Wh-what's wrong?"

"Honey, you said last night your father wasn't a nice man. Will you tell me about it?"

"Wh-why do you want to know? And he wasn't my father. He was my sperm donor." He nodded, trying to give her a smile.

"I watched my brother pretty deep in conversation with your mom. It's a twin thing, but I'm pretty sure she was telling him a story that I need to hear as well, and I'd sure like to hear it from you, Keegan." She nibbled on that bottom lip, and he desperately wanted to take it between his teeth and do the nibbling for her. Instead, he gripped his thighs, holding his hands flat down, away from her body.

"M-my mom got pregnant at eighteen. I told you that. He was a member of a motorcycle gang, the Desert Bastards," she said.

"Oh fuck," he moaned.

"Yea, they... my mom thinks she was drugged that first night. I wouldn't put it past them. I was a kid, and some of the shit they said to me... it-it was awful. There were club whores all around, giving blow jobs any time, day or night, fucking on pool tables. It didn't matter that a little girl was wandering around."

"Did you guys try to leave?" She nodded, wiping a tear on her cheek.

"So many times. Every time he pulled Mom back. He beat her, and then one day, he beat me." Ryan's hands fisted on his thighs, and he clenched his jaw. "He was hitting Mom so hard, and I tried to step in. He gripped my ponytail and threw me against the wall, then he slapped me. I just remember my mom screaming. He said I was going to make him a lot of money as part of his stable when I turned fourteen. Until then, he said I had to learn respect, so-so he cut off all my hair."

"Fuck, baby," he growled. Ryan couldn't take it anymore. Scooting closer to Keegan, he pulled her body against his, rubbing circles on her back. She stiffened at first and then melted into the big strong arms of Ryan. His body felt so safe, so secure, and she let the tears flow. When she finally caught her breath, she leaned back.

"Th-this woman, her husband had been killed in the club, she helped us. Mom just drove and drove, but if he ever finds us... finds her... he'll kill her, Ryan. He won't give her any mercy at all. He might kidnap me and sell me, but he'll kill Mom." Ryan let a big, callused thumb brush away her tears.

"He won't touch either one of you, honey. You have my word." He leaned forward and kissed the tip of her nose. Keegan let out a long hot breath, stunned. "I'm s-sorry…" She shook her head and then leaned forward, pressing her lips against his.

For Ryan, it was the single most perfect kiss in his entire life. Her lips were full and sweet, molding perfectly to his own, her hot breath mixed with his own. Pulling her against his body, she straddled his thighs, wrapping her arms around his shoulders, the kiss deeper. He finally gathered his senses and pulled back.

"Fucking hell, Keegan, that was amazing, baby, but we need to slow down." She started to say something, and he held a finger to her lips. "I want to slow down, honey. You're worth it. I want to go slow with you, Keegan. I like you more than I fucking should, but I like you a lot. I want to get to know you and have a million more kisses like that. The old me? The old me would have you against the wall fucking your brains out right now. The Ryan that wants to see where this goes? He's going to take his time. You good with that, baby?" Keegan smiled down at Ryan, her hands still cupping his face. She placed a sweet kiss on his lips, and he moaned, rubbing his hard dick against her heat.

"I'm good with that, Ryan, thank you."

"Don't thank me, baby. I might be dead from blue balls by morning." She laughed, standing from his lap, noticing the outline of the long thick ridge in his jeans.

"I think you're being a tad dramatic, but I understand. What do we do now?" she asked.

"We have to tell Ghost," he said. "He's the president of our club and our team lead. I trust him with every life in this building."

"I understand. What about me and mom? Should we leave?" she asked. Pulling Keegan into his own body, his arms wrapped around her.

"Baby girl, you're not fucking going anywhere without me. It won't be easy, Keegan. I have a past, and it shows up here almost every Friday and Saturday night. I'm more than fucking sorry it's going to do that, but know that it's just that, my past." She nodded, grinning.

"I have a past too, Ryan. It might show up here, or somewhere else we go. But I've never, never cheated on someone I care for, and I hate to say this, but I care for you more than I should."

"I'm fucking glad to hear that, honey. Although, if things really work out, our family reunions are going to be seriously fucked up."

CHAPTER NINE

"The fucking Desert Bastards," said Ghost through clenched teeth. "Of all the fucking clubs on the planet. Those assholes have been chafing my ass for at least five years now."

"I-I'm so sorry," said Tinley tentatively. "I tried to tell, Ty; we'll leave." Zulu shook his head, staring at the mother-daughter duo.

"Nope," he said, grinning. "That's not what Ghost meant. You're family now, both of you, at least I'm pretty damn sure both of you are." Zulu laughed as Ty gripped Tinley's hand, and Ryan gripped Keegan's.

"That isn't what I meant," said Ghost. "Listen, our club, we work to stop human trafficking, and the name of the Bastards has come across our radar one too many times in the last few years. They're not only running a bunch of prostitution rings. They're kidnapping and selling young girls here in the U.S. as well as Mexico. We want to stop them, but if we go after them, that might put a spotlight on you two."

"Oh God," whispered Tinley, "I think... I think we should leave... go somewhere..."

"No, you're not going anywhere, honey," said Ty. "Nowhere safer than right here, Tinley. Nowhere. You can't keep running from this man. We have to figure out how to stop him and stop the club."

"B-but they're huge," she said, looking at the table.

"Not anymore," said Ghost. "You may not have heard, but five years ago, they had a huge blowout. Half the club took off to other clubs, the other half sort of fell apart. They discovered that their president was cooking the books." Tinley bit her bottom lip and nodded.

"Fuck, you knew?" said Whiskey.

"I was doing the books for him. He was asking me to cover the profits. I didn't say anything to anyone, but if he finds me, he'll think I leaked that information."

"Not gonna happen, honey," said Gunner.

"Mom," whispered Keegan, "I-I think we should trust them. I want to have a life, Mom. A life where I'm not looking over my shoulder all the time."

"Oh, Keegan, honey, what I have done?" she cried.

"Mom," she said, pulling her mother in for a hug, "you haven't done anything. You've protected me for fifteen years, Mom, fifteen years! You've given me a life I could have only dreamed of before. All I'm saying is, I'm saying there's another life waiting for me, for you, I think, in this room." Keegan looked up at Ryan, and he plastered a big smile on his face. Tinley nodded.

"What do we need to do?" asked Tinley.

"We're going to make a plan," said Ghost. "First thing we need to do is track down this Brick guy. You may not want to hear this, but we will eliminate him."

"E-eliminate him?" she croaked, looking at her daughter.

"He's my sperm donor, doesn't bother me at all," said Keegan. Ryan laughed, nodding at her.

"That's why I'm crazy about you, Keegan." The whole room stilled, smiling at Ryan. Never in his time with them had he ever said anything so romantically sweet. His twin beamed and dipped his chin at him.

"S-so, what do I do? Do you need me to draw him out?"

"No fucking way," growled Ty. "We will handle this, honey. Men like him don't usually have enough common sense to hide. They're usually in plain sight, thinking they're too smart to get caught, except they're not. We have some good contacts in Vegas. We'll find him." She nodded, gripping his fingers tighter.

"Wh-what about your families? You have wives who are pregnant, children. I can't let..." Ghost held up his hand, smiling, looking at the room.

"Any of you assholes ever notice how every woman we bring into our fold is worried about the other women and children?" They all laughed and nodded. "Lesson for everyone else, the first woman you bring here who doesn't show that kind of concern is the wrong woman. Tinley, this is a fortified complex. The gates and fences can be electrified, the steel doors are bulletproof, the steel wall separating the restaurant from the barn is fifteen inches thick and buried twenty feet down. No one, and I do mean no one, is going to get through here."

"Which brings us to another point," said Tango. "It might be a good idea for you two to stay here for a while."

"But... but I have a job," she said.

"Mom, you can do your job from home. You've done it before. Tell the firm that you've got something contagious, and you're housebound for a while. There's no reason for you to go in." Tinley nodded at her daughter.

"What about you? What about the salon?"

"I don't know. Maybe, could I maybe use the cottage on the property as a temporary salon? Maybe put a sign on my doors that I have a gas leak or something?"

"I think that's a great idea," said Ryan. "We can even stay in the cottage since it's been brought into the fence line since Charlie stayed there." Keegan smiled at him, her stomach doing that funny butterfly dance. Sleep there together? Was she ready for that?

"Sounds like you guys have thought of everything," said Tinley.

"It's what we do, Tinley," said Ghost, smiling. Ace sat at the end of the table, pecking away, and then looked up.

"Fuck," he murmured.

"Oh shit, what is that 'fuck' for?" asked Razor. He turned the computer for the room to see pictures of the New Year's Eve party. Three pictures in the center of the Facebook page for Valerie included Tinley and Ty, and the others had Ryan and Keegan.

"I have a program that runs facial recognition on social media sites. I know you said you didn't have one, but people catch others in their photos all the time," he said, looking at Keegan as she strained to read the text thread.

"What did she post?" asked Keegan, outraged. She read the lines slowly. "This skank whore blocked my cock tonight. Won't happen again, bitch." The room inhaled a deep breath and waited. Ryan, to his credit, flushed a deep crimson.

"You really have shit taste in women," she said, grinning at him. Ryan let out the breath he was holding and shook his head.

"I DID have shit taste in women. Past tense. DID," he grinned.

"Good answer, big guy," she said, kissing his cheek. Ghost chuckled and shook his head.

"Okay, Ace, try to get that shit off the internet. Whiskey? Track down this asshole Brick. Zulu? Reach out to the boys at the Vegas Aces and the Reno Riders. See if they know anything about what's happening out there. Hawk and Eagle go with Tinley and Keegan to gather whatever they need for here. Set up Keegan in the cottage. Stay with her. Do not leave her side. Eagle? You can stay here in the suites, or you can use the cabin on the property."

"We'll talk about it," he said to his boss. Ghost nodded and rapped his knuckles on the table.

"Let's go finish this shit."

CHAPTER TEN

Pulling into the driveway of the small house where Tinley and Keegan lived, Skull stayed with the vehicle while Hawk and Eagle followed the women inside. Hawk said something to Keegan, then turned and walked back to his friend.

"Hey, man," Skull held up a hand, smiling.

"It's not a big deal, Hawk, really. We had fun, but for her, there wasn't anything sexual there. I certainly would have fucked her. I won't lie, but I didn't see her as long-term. She's nice, Hawk, really nice, so don't fuck it up, brother." Hawk nodded.

"I've been hearing that a lot lately," he said, turning back to look at the house. "I like her, Skull, really like her, and it scares the fuck out of me." His friend nodded, grinning.

"That's a sure-fire sign, brother. Hold on to your shorts; you're about to be hit by a boulder." Hawk chuckled under his breath, heading back into the house. It was small with a nice open living and kitchen space. The house was clean, other than Keegan's room which reminded him way too much of his own room back at the barn.

"I see you and I have the same maid," he joked. Keegan turned around with a cute blush, shaking her head.

"Yea, it's one of my many bad habits. Ironically, my workplace is spotless. I'm crazy about the neatness of my salon and making sure everything is sanitized. My room? Not so much." She moved toward her dresser, pulling out various articles of clothing, and when she got to the top drawer with her bras and panties, she casually tossed them into the suitcase. Hawk couldn't help but smile at the variety of lace thongs and bras that matched.

"You like to coordinate," he grinned. "Very sexy, Keegan."

"What? You don't coordinate your boxers and your t-shirts?" she smiled.

"No," he laughed, folding his arms across his chest. "Most days, I don't wear boxers." That got a blush out of Keegan, who continued tossing things in the bags.

"Okay, I think that's all I need. We'll need to run by the shop and let my assistant know that we'll be moving temporarily. I can gather everything I need there." He nodded, lifting the two large bags off her bed. The whole room smelled like Keegan, fresh and spicy. "Hawk? Do you think... do you think he'll come for us?"

"I don't know, baby," he said, looking down at her. "What I do know is that between my brother and I, and all those other men, they won't get to you. I won't let them, Keegan, I promise." She nodded as he leaned down and pressed a kiss to her forehead. His lips were warm and soft, the scent of his soap filling her senses.

"Mom? Do you have everything?" she called. Her mother's bedroom door was shut, and the two of them smirked.

"A-almost. Be out in a few."

"Let's take this out. Knowing my brother, they may be a few minutes."

Tinley laughed against Ty's chest, her legs still wrapped around his waist while he was buried inside her, his hot, stiff cock pulsing against her walls.

"Damn, you feel good, baby girl," he moaned. "I needed to have you again, honey, have you in your bed. Last time, though." Tinley's eyes went wide with shock.

"Wh-what? What did I do?" Ty pulled back, looking at her.

"Tinley, baby, I mean, it's the last time you'll be in this bed. Going forward, you're going to be sharing my bed, honey, not be alone in this one. Clear?" She nodded, biting that lower lip he loved so much. He noticed Keegan had the same habit, although on her, it did nothing to his libido.

"S-sorry... I thought..."

"I know what you thought, baby girl," he said, lifting her knee higher, pressing into her harder and harder, "stop thinking like that. Let me spell it out, honey. Fuck, you feel good. Spelling it out, I love you, Tinley, love you, baby." Ty never stopped his assault on her wet pussy, slamming his big dick in and out as she clutched his shoulders.

"Oh... oh, God... Ty... I... I love you too. This is crazy. Shit, I'm cumming..." she moaned as his own orgasm began with a deep vibration throughout his body, his load spilling inside her once again. Gasping for air, he leaned against her forehead.

"Say it again," he whispered.

"Say... oh," she smiled, "I love you too, Ty. I'm scared to death, but I know what I'm feeling. I love you too." He kissed her with a passion she'd never felt before, this giant of a man hovering above her, the body and face of a god. "We better get out there, or they're going to leave us."

After leaving their rental house, Keegan stopped at her salon to pick up her supplies and let her assistant know she was off for the next week but would get paid her regular salary. Coming out of the salon, Ryan and Keegan ran straight into Valerie and Cheri, the same women who'd shared their photos on their social media pages.

"Well, well, well, looks like his cock liked your pussy," said Valerie, sneering at Keegan. "He never lets anybody hang out for more than a few hours."

"Enough, Valerie," growled Ryan. "I never lied to you. You knew the score and were more than happy to spread your legs for me, or, I might add, for any brother who wanted you."

"Yea, I knew the score, does she? Does she know you'll fuck her and leave her? Does she know what a freak you are?" Ryan never laid a hand on a woman in anger in his life, but he was sorely tempted to, taking a half step forward. Keegan lay her hand on his arm and smiled.

"I don't know you, and you don't know me. You have no clue what kind of woman I am. Maybe I'm a little freaky too. But from your actions, I know what kind of woman you are. It's fine to party and have a good time. Hell, we've all done it, but when someone doesn't want to party with you anymore, don't blame them, blame yourself."

"Oh, I don't blame him," she sneered, "I blame you. He just needs to wet his dick, is all. He'll realize in no time that only we can give him what he wants and needs. Right, Cheri?" Her friend looked at Ryan and then back at Keegan, an expression that said "I'm sorry" filled her face.

"I don't know, Val. I mean, it was all in good fun. We meet lots of guys…"

"Shut up!" yelled Val. Cheri shook her head and walked in the other direction, leaving her friend to fend for herself. "You're gonna regret leaving me, baby. You know you will."

"What I regret," said Ryan, "is ever starting anything with you in the first place. Leave it alone, Val. We're done, and nothing will change that." He gripped Keegan's hand and pulled her toward the truck. Tucking her safely inside, he stowed her supplies and then crawled up beside her.

There was silence in the vehicle as they drove, no one saying anything. Ryan's stomach was in knots, the fear of Keegan not speaking to him ever again. He looked out the window, willing the emotions to go back down until she reached out, lacing her fingers with his. Looking down at their intertwined hands, Ryan nearly burst out crying. As he looked up, she smiled at him, giving him a wink.

"Told you. You had terrible taste in women," she said quietly. Ryan broke out in nervous laughter, the knot that was constricting in his chest loosening. He nodded and smiled at her. But it was the look of pride his own brother gave him that nearly undid him.

Had he really been such a dick that he'd used women, traded his soul for a few minutes of pleasure, all so he would feel more complete? When the truth of it all was, he was feeling less complete every time he took a woman to bed. The feeling he'd had when looking at Keegan walking into the bar was growing inside him, the feeling of wholeness, of completion, and it was a feeling he did not want to lose.

"Home, James," said Keegan, smiling. "Or I guess Scott."

"Yes, ma'am, home it is."

CHAPTER ELEVEN

As Keegan and Ryan made the cottage comfortable for the two of them, they enjoyed cooking and sharing a meal together, laughing about silly things, and finally settling on a movie they could both agree on. When the movie finished, Keegan, who was leaning against Ryan's big body, rose and smiled.

"Well, I guess I'll head to bed," she grinned. "Thanks for today, Ryan. Really."

He nodded, watching her move toward her bedroom. He'd never actually slept near a woman without *sleeping* with her, although that was a lie too. He'd never slept beside a woman in his life. Valerie was right about that. He'd fucked plenty and then either pushed them out the door or he walked out.

His head was brought back to what Keegan said that first night. He did have mommy issues, and maybe he needed to speak with Bree. His mother leaving them at such a young age without explanation was definitely hard on both he and Ty, although obviously, his brother handled it much better.

Walking into the second bedroom, he stripped out of his clothes, pulling on the warm flannel pants and a t-shirt. Normally, he would sleep in the nude, but one, Keegan was just across the hall, and two, it was freezing outside. If the weather reports were correct, another blizzard was headed their way.

Unable to sleep, he grabbed one of the books off the shelf, something about travel, and started to scan the pages. A few minutes later, he heard the soft padding of footsteps and

Keegan standing in the doorway of his room. She was dressed similar to him, except with a camisole instead of t-shirt. The thin material molded against her breasts, the cold forcing her huge button nipples to poke through.

"You okay, honey?" he asked.

"I-I'm scared. Can I lay with you?" Fucking hell, yep, he was paying for his man-whoring ways.

"Of course, you can. Come here." He pulled the covers back, allowing her to slip inside. Immediately, her cold feet nudged his legs, and he shivered. "Fuck! Honey, you're freezing."

"I d-don't think the heat works in that room," she said, burrowing further into the blankets.

"No problem," he smiled. "Come here. I won't do anything, I promise, Keegan, but let me just hold you and get you warm." She nodded as he pulled her into his arms, the warmth of the steely muscles enveloping her in safety and heat. Her head was tucked beneath his chin, their lower legs hooked around one another.

When she was finally warm, she pulled back to stare at his face. Her hands were lying flat against one another as if she were praying. Ryan slid one of his big hands below hers and the other above. Their foreheads were touching, their lips just inches apart.

"Tell me the stupidest thing you've ever done," she whispered. He chuckled.

"How much time do we have because it's a big list. Not sure I could pick one thing." She waited patiently until he finally spoke. "Okay, so Valerie ranks up there for sure. I knew she was crazy, but, well, when a woman agrees to do just about anything to your body, you sort of lose all common sense. Fucking the forty-four-year-old neighbor lady when I was seventeen was the other."

"A case of Mrs. Robinson?" she smiled.

"Something like that. She was known for her 'work' with the youth of the area. I definitely bought into it. What made it more stupid was that I snuck in her window while her husband, a Marine, was in the other room. If my father, also a Marine, had known, he would have been so disappointed in me."

"Wow, you really do like to live dangerously, don't you?"

"Stupidly, not dangerously. I think the stupidest thing I ever did at work was probably puffing out my chest against Ghost, trying to show him how good I was. Not smart."

"He is kind of intimidating," she whispered. "I mean, you're all big men, but he seems, I don't know, big in size and personality and something else."

"Yea, that's Ghost. It's why he's the leader. I'm lucky he gave me a shot. Lucky for Ty too. I could have fucked it up for him, and I damn sure didn't want that to happen. What about you? Stupidest thing you ever did?" he asked.

"Hmmm, I'd have to say going home with a man I didn't even know. I was nineteen and feeling a bit rebellious. He picked me up in a bar, a bar I shouldn't have legally been in. I was drunk, and he convinced me we should go to his house."

"What happened, baby?"

"He... I knew it was stupid right away. His house was really dark, and I got nervous and said I needed to use the ladies' room. He had a playroom. It was across from the bathroom."

"A playroom? As in BDSM?"

"Yep," she said, looking into his eyes, "not my finest hour. I was lucky the bathroom window was big enough for me to crawl out. I don't know what he would have done, but I wasn't going to wait around and find out."

"I'm sorry that happened to you, honey. A little spanking and things like that can be fun, but not if both partners aren't willing." She nodded and pulled herself an inch closer to him, feeling his heat.

"Ryan?"

"Yea, baby?"

"Will you kiss me again?" she asked, looking into his eyes.

"Honey, I want nothing more, but I'm not sure I can stop once I start."

"I trust you, please, just kiss me," she begged.

Hawk steeled himself to act like the man his father would want him to be. Placing his hands on either side of her face, he gently leaned forward, touching his own lips to hers. With a heavy sigh, she melted into him, and Ryan pulled her body tighter into his own.

"Touch me," she whispered, taking his hand, guiding it down her pajama pants. Ryan let his fingers glide down her flat, taut belly, the feel of her soft curls making him groan. He was painfully hard, and it was nearly impossible for her to not feel him against her thigh. Sliding a

finger inside her wet, tight opening, he nearly came in his own pants.

"Baby girl," he gasped, "you're so fucking wet for me."

"Yes, Ryan, for you. All for you," she moaned as his fingers scissored inside her, her

body instantly reacting to his touch.

Ryan had never felt so powerful in all his years. He held this woman's pleasure literally

in his hands, and that was something he'd never given a second thought to before. As she

rocked against him, releasing a loud cry of satisfaction, he pulled his fingers from her, placing

them in his mouth, licking each one with gratification.

"You taste so fucking good, Keegan," he said, kissing her. She reached down to grip his

rigid cock, and he shook his head. "Not tonight, baby. Tonight, was about you. We have all the

time in the world, honey."

"A-are you sure?" she asked, surprised.

"Positive. That was the hottest fucking thing I've ever done. Let me have that, and you

get some sleep. I'm watching over you. We're safe, baby girl." She nodded, already half asleep

as he pulled the comforters up over their bodies.

Ryan lay awake for nearly an hour, just watching her sleep, her soft little snorts the

cutest damn thing he'd ever seen. He brushed his fingers through her hair, let his hands

wander over her fully clothed curves, smiling at the miracle of his feelings.

This was love. This is what Ty and Tinley were feeling. This is what all of his brothers

were feeling. Holy fuck, I'm in love.

CHAPTER TWELVE

Ty and Tinley woke to the pre-dawn sounds of howling winds, snow flying across the windows, little ice crystals hitting the glass. She burrowed into the covers as his hot body snuggled against her.

"Doesn't look like anyone is going anywhere today," he smiled.

"No, do you think Keegan and Ryan are okay? I mean, I know they're okay, but will they be okay in the cottage alone?"

Ty smiled down at her, placing a kiss at the corner of her mouth. A few weeks ago, he would have said they needed to send a search party and get Keegan out of that cottage with his whoring brother. Now, after seeing his reactions yesterday with Val, he was certain of the direction that relationship was headed.

"I think they'll be just fine. All of our phones are working, and worst-case scenario, we can hike to the cottage and get them or send them supplies. It's not all that far, just tucked out of the way."

"Will you tell me more about you? Where you grew up?" she asked.

"In case you haven't figured it out, Tinley, I'll tell you anything, my precious girl," he grinned, kissing the top of her head. "We were born in Illinois but moved to San Diego when we were babies. Our dad was in the Marine Corps as well. Mom left us when we were six. No notes, no explanations, nothing. She just was gone one day, and Dad suddenly became mom and dad."

"That's awful," she said with compassion.

"It wasn't so bad. We didn't understand, but Dad was awesome. He was the most patient, kind man on the planet. He was already pretty high ranking at the time, but he was able to get assigned permanently to the base outside San Diego, so we wouldn't be left alone."

"Ryan, Ry really struggled when Mom left. I think he just believed that all women would abandon him, so he'd abandon them first."

"That makes sense given his history with women. Never getting too close, never allowing them the option to leave him. He needed to speak to someone," said Tinley. Ty nodded, his brow furrowed with worry lines.

"I thought I would be enough for him. I mean, we're twins, so we shared everything. I kept his secrets, covered for him. Maybe I shouldn't have."

"You can't think like that, honey. You have no idea how he would have reacted if you hadn't been there. I think you did what was in your nature. You protected him." Ty nodded, kissing her once more.

"When we graduated from high school, Ryan immediately went off and joined the Marine Corps with me in tow. I couldn't let him join alone, so I signed up too. I think he planned it all, the little bastard," he grinned. "We stayed in five years and then left to come here with Ghost."

"And your dad?" she asked.

"He died that last year of our service. He was older when we were born, almost forty-seven. Mom was just twenty-nine, so maybe, maybe, she wanted a younger man."

"That's not it at all," said Tinley. "She was a selfish woman, Ty, a woman who wanted it all and realized she couldn't have it. You two were lucky to have your dad for as long as you did. My parents... when they found out I was pregnant and dropping out of college, they called me every name in the book. I've thought about that moment so many times. I swore I would never treat a child of mine that way."

"And you haven't, honey," he said, grinning. "Look at the way you treat Keegan. You let her make her own decisions and mistakes but don't condemn her for them."

"Yea, you're right there. God, my dad was awful to me. When I called my grandmother, who lived a few towns over, she welcomed me with open arms. She said my parents were hypocrites considering my mom was pregnant when they got married. It explained a lot about their loveless marriage."

"We won't have a loveless marriage, baby, not us. There's too much fire and passion between me and you. Besides the fact that I respect and admire the fuck outta you. Won't happen to us, honey." She leaned up on one elbow and kissed him, tasting his morning breath.

"You know that my only experience with men was Keegan's father..."

"Sperm donor. She said so," he grinned.

"Yes," she laughed, "sperm donor. I don't even remember that first night, and I was a virgin. After that... he would..."

"Precious girl, you do not have to tell me any of this if you don't want to."

"I know. I just think you should know. He would screw all those club whores and still come and find me at night. Keegan and I shared a room alone, but he would come in. I didn't want her to wake up, so I would comply. The thing was, for all his talk about what he did with the whores, he never did anything out of the norm with me. He would either just bend me over a chair or force me to lie there in missionary position."

"I'm so fucking sorry, baby," he said, kissing her.

"Don't be. You've taught me more about making love, not having sex, in the last week than he did in seven years. Because of you, Ty, I know what it is for a man to make love to me."

"Fuck, baby," he pulled her close, kissing her.

"I'd like to... I'd like to be a little, ummm, adventurous with you. Can we do that?" Ty's eyes grew wide as he looked down into the blue/green waves of hers.

"What do you mean, baby?"

"I want you to fuck me... in my ass," she said plainly. He tried to control the rock-hard erection he was now sporting but just couldn't.

"I'm a big man, honey. You've seen me. We're gonna have to work our way up to that," he grinned.

"I know. I want to, I want to feel that. I also want you to shoot all over me, let me lick it off our bodies, take me in the shower, fuck me in a semi-public place, tear my clothes off me..."

"Whoa, whoa, whoa," he laughed. "Where is all this coming from?" She blushed a bright red, and it suddenly dawned on him. "Oh shit. Charlie. You found out who Charlie is and read some of her books."

"Okay, in my defense, I already read the first one, but yes, when I found out who she was, the girls gave me the rest of them. I really like them, Ty I mean, the women in those books are strong and adventurous and not scared to let their men show them new things. I want to be that woman... with you. I want to keep your interest for the next fifty years."

"Tinley, baby girl, look at me," he said, sitting up in the bed. "If you and I only ever had sex like we have the last few days, I would be happy with you for the next fifty years. Variety is fun, baby, no doubt, but this, you and me, this is about more than sex. Now, I'm more than willing to explore with you and try new things at your pace. But make no mistake, my girl, nothing will ever make me get bored or tired of you, nothing."

"What if I turn gray?"

"Won't matter, baby. What if I go bald?" he asked, grinning at her.

"It doesn't matter as much to women if a man loses his hair or turns gray," she smiled. "I mean, I'm going to have wrinkles before you."

"Honey, look at me. I'm twenty-seven years old, and I already have lines and wrinkles because of the amount of time I've spent in the sun, the life I've lived. You barely have a crinkle around your eyes. If people stood us side-by-side, Tinley, they would think we're the same age. Stop obsessing, baby. It. Does. Not. Matter."

"Okay, okay, no more obsessing about our age. Now, will you please, please play with my ass," she grinned.

"Fuck yea, I will!" Ty brought his mouth down to taste her, her fingers laced through his hair as his tongue went to work on her pussy. Just as she was about to scream out in pleasure, he flipped her onto her stomach. With one big arm beneath her hips, he tilted her up. Spreading her cheeks, his tongue found its way between her folds, one thick, rough thumb circling her hole.

Sliding his thumb in her pussy for lubrication, he pulled out and gently pressed into her. She was so damn tight his dick immediately jumped, small bits of cum coating his big head. Moaning, he slid in further as his tongue flicked in and out of her.

"Oh, Ty, that feels so amazing, oh, honey…"

He grinned against her lips, his tongue plunging inside her as he continued to force his thumb in and out, the sounds of her moaning nearly his undoing. He could feel it coming for her, her walls contracting around his thumb and tongue. Arching her back, she let out a cry of pleasure, falling into the sheets.

Turning, Ty was still kneeling above her, his thick cock bobbing up and down, the almost painful-looking purple head staring at her. She reached out to touch him, but he shook his head, rubbing his cock up and down, his big thumb still covered in her juices slicking over the tip.

Tinley spread her legs wide, so he could move closer, and she knew the minute he was going to unload on her. His face contorted in a spasm of pleasure and pain, the hot juices squirting all over her belly. She sat up, immediately placing his sensitive head inside her mouth to taste the last remnants of his orgasm. Her stomach covered in his desire, she let her fingers glide across, scooping up a big line of sticky cum, sucking him off her fingers.

"Fucking hell, baby girl, that was the hottest shit ever," he said, falling to the bed. "We don't need anything to spice up our sex life, honey. That was amazing."

"It was pretty awesome," she grinned. "I want to do that again." Ty laughed at her, nodding.

"You might be older, baby, but I'm gonna need a minute." Tinley smiled down at him, pulling the blankets up behind her as she lay against his naked flesh.

"You might need a minute," she grinned as she kissed her way down his chest to that beautiful deep vee of his pelvis, "but I don't, so let me help you get there." Ty looked down at the head of hair, now sucking his cock with vigor. He grinned, placing his hands behind his head.

"Yes, ma'am…"

CHAPTER THIRTEEN

As the blizzard raged outside, the team gathered in the restaurant to discuss what they'd found out about the Desert Bastards.

"Whiskey? What did you discover?" asked Ghost.

"Brick, Ralph Tolbert, is a grade A piece of shit," he mumbled. Tinley let a bit of laughter slip out and nodded at the man, his serious expression softening somewhat as she did. "He has an arrest record that would make Charles Manson blush. Five times arrested for aggravated assault, three times on suspicion of murder, twice for alleged kidnapping, and a total of ten charges for drug possession, all thrown out due to lack of evidence or witnesses refusing to testify."

"That sounds like him," said Tinley, swallowing. "He was always getting into fights and always trying to force drugs on me." Whiskey nodded.

"That's the other thing. The cops all believe he's running a group of young women out of a house somewhere in or around Vegas. Men are basically ordering the women over the phone; they get delivered to a hotel room for a specific amount of time and then are picked up again. A guy called the cops anonymously, of course, and reported that he believed the girl they sent him was seriously underage. His estimate was twelve or thirteen."

"Oh my God," whispered Grace.

"He claimed he didn't touch the girl but that she had needle marks on her arm and bruises on her body. He was going to get her somewhere safe, but there was a man standing outside his room the entire time. He gave the cops the number he called, but it was disconnected when they tried it."

"Burner phones," said Ace. "They're using burners, so they aren't traced. Probably use a different one every time." Whiskey nodded in agreement.

"I'm pretty sure that's right. Two months ago, some hikers in the desert found a woman's body. She was naked, beaten, and definitely had track marks on her arms and on her feet. It was estimated that she was between sixteen and twenty, although they couldn't be sure. She…" Whiskey looked up at the women, and they all nodded for him to continue. "She had no teeth for them to get any impressions."

"That poor girl," said Keegan. "That man… that man is my…"

"He's your nothing, honey," said Ryan. "Like you said, he's your sperm donor. You are not him." She nodded, nuzzling closer to him, wrapped in a big shawl, trying to stave off the cold.

"When I asked what they were doing about it, the local PD said they were working with the Feds to stop it."

"Ivan?" asked Ghost.

"I've left him a message. It would seem if there's trafficking and drugs involved, Ivan would know something." Ghost nodded and turned toward Zulu.

"What did the Riders and the Aces say?"

"Riders say they know about Brick but that he hasn't been stupid enough to come into their territory. When the Bastards were disbanded, their president, Dawg, disappeared. He stole enough money to go anywhere he wanted to, but they don't think he left the area. The others completely scattered. He said three approached him about joining their club, but they were so high on their own shit he wanted nothing to do with them.

"Six men went to Mexico. He knows that for sure and has kept eyes on them. The rest of the men either gave up riding with a club and became Nomads or simply walked off the face of the earth. The Aces are another story. They claim there are a few hanging around, most notably Brick. He kept a few of the older guys on with him and runs primarily heroin and cocaine from Mexico, through Nevada, and then out to Oakland to get it on the ships. Knuckles says about a year ago, they were trying to find a missing girl. Sixteen, cheerleader, prom queen, the whole nine yards. Single mom reported her missing after she went to the movies with her friends."

"I don't think I'm going to like this," said Ghost.

"You're not. Her friends said she walked toward the bus stop, and that was the last they saw of her. Four weeks later, they found her. She was standing on a street corner so strung out she couldn't even tell them her name. Her hair was cut and dyed; she was malnourished to the point of almost emaciated, body had been so abused they were shocked she could even stand. By the time they got her to the emergency room, she'd coded and died."

"Those poor parents," whispered Bree.

"Yea, well, it wasn't the last. It seems his pattern. He's kidnapping girls from all over the place, getting them hooked on the drugs, then pimping them out. These girls are so young they have no clue where to go or where to run to. Knuckles thinks the house he's keeping them in must be out in the middle of nowhere if these girls aren't running to neighbors or neighbors aren't calling the cops."

"Unfortunately, that makes sense," said Ace. "What about credit cards? Bank accounts? Anything we can trace back to this guy? Did he have family?" he asked, looking at Tinley.

"No," she said, shaking her head. "Other than the club, he had no one that I was aware of."

"Then that's where he's getting help. Someone from the club. Would Dawg help him?" he asked.

"H-he might. I mean, Dawg was the president, but he was definitely cheating the entire club out of money that should have been shared. Brick always liked him, though, protected him, I guess."

"Then maybe he liked him enough to work with him again," said Ace. "Let me check into some things, and we can go from there."

"I think once we get all the information we need, we're going to need to make a trip to Nevada," said Zulu. "I don't want to, but we may be able to find this guy and put an end to him."

"Agreed," said Ghost. "Alright, everyone, with the storm, we've closed the shop, the Club, and the clinic is only open for emergencies. Weather reports say this is gonna last a few days, so hunker down and stay warm and safe. If anyone needs help chopping firewood, let us know, and we'll all chip in. Hawk? Cottage okay?"

"I don't think the heat is working in part of the house," he said, "but we've just moved to one side, and all seems to be fine. I have plenty of firewood, so all is good."

"I've cancelled all my clients for the rest of the week," said Keegan. "I won't see anyone for at least another five days."

"Good, and you Tinley?"

"I called the firm and told them I needed a leave of absence, family emergency. They weren't thrilled with it but couldn't deny me since I'm a partner. I've taken sixty days off, just to be sure."

"Great," he said, smiling. "Eagle? You're good with all this?"

"I'm not good that the woman I'm in love with is in danger," he smiled at his teammates, "but I'm damn sure good with the fact that I have a woman I'm in love with."

The room erupted in cheers and applause. Tinley blushed and buried her face in his chest. She glanced at her daughter, who was looking at Ryan in the same way she looked at Ty.

"So, wait," said Axe. "If you marry Tinley, and Hawk marries Keegan, does that mean she's your stepdaughter and your sister-in-law, and, Hawk, does that mean she's your mother-in-law and your sister-in-law?"

"I think I have a headache," said Ice, grinning.

"It sounds about right," smiled Ty. "Let's just say it will be complicated but perfectly legal."

"Alright, everyone, stay in communication and stay safe and warm. Ty? Will you guys be moving to the cabin?"

"Not right now," he said, smiling at Tinley. "We're fine in my rooms." The team, their wives, and children dispersed headed back to their own homes. As Tinley looked up at Ty, she felt a warmth flood through her body that had never been there before.

"You okay, baby?" he asked.

"Never better. I'm in love with you, Ty, truly, madly, deeply in love with you." Ty picked her up in his arms as she let out a peal of laughter.

"Show me."

CHAPTER FOURTEEN

Keegan stomped her feet in the mudroom of the cottage, the chunks of snow falling on the weathered rug. Hanging her scarf and jacket, beside her Ryan did the same. Stepping into the living room, he placed a few more logs on the fire and stoked the embers, flames rising up to immediately heat the room again.

"I'll start some soup for dinner. Does that sound okay?" she asked.

"Sounds perfect, babe." Ryan grinned to himself at the sounds of domestication around him. Who would have thought he'd like this kind of life? A life with one woman, alone in a cottage for days on end.

Placing all the ingredients in a pot to simmer, Keegan lowered the flame and then moved to sit on the sofa next to Ryan. Her feet were still clad in heavy wool socks. She pulled the blanket around her and snuggled next to him.

"You want to play one of those board games on the shelf?" he asked.

"No, I'd rather hear more about you," she smiled.

"Okay, but question for a question," he said. Nodding, Keegan sat cross-legged beside him, their fingers linked.

"You first," he said.

"Okay, if you hadn't gone into the Marines, what would you have done?"

"Great question," he said, raising a brow. "Dad saved for us to go to college, so when we joined, he put that money aside for us to use later. I never really wanted to be anything except a Marine, but I'm pretty sure Ty did. If we're just talking about me, though, I think I would have become a teacher."

"Wow! Really?" surprise spread on her face. He nodded.

"Yep. I love the idea of changing a mind, making someone see something that wasn't there before."

"Like you did with me and you," she said, kissing his lips. Chuckling, he nodded once again.

"My turn. I know your childhood probably sucked before you got away, but what was it like afterwards?"

"Yea, Mom really shielded me as much as she could at the club. She would tell me these stories that always made me believe everything would be okay. For the most part, the guys were nice to me. There were a few that would say things like, 'she's gonna be a great piece when she's older.' I didn't understand, but I heard, and I remember. Afterwards, Mom worked so hard, and there wasn't a lot of money, but she always created adventures for us. We would pack peanut butter and jelly sandwiches and go sit by a lake and just stare at the clouds, guessing what they looked like."

"She sounds like an amazing Mom," he said with a hard swallow.

"She was... is. When I told her I didn't want to go to college, she simply nodded and said, 'no problem, so what are you going to do with your life?' I knew I loved hair and make-up, so I got my cosmetology license, as well as my esthetician's license. I worked for someone else for two years, saving every penny I made to buy that little shop in town. Mom helps me manage my books, and I'm finally at a place where I can pay myself a decent salary."

"You're unbelievable, honey," he said, pulling her in for a hug.

"My turn," she smiled. "You are obviously very experienced with sex, but what haven't you done that you want to do?" Oh, fuck no, this had trap written all over it. Shit, shit, shit. "Ryan, I'm not judging you. I'm asking for me."

"What do you mean?"

"I mean, I want to know what you haven't done with another woman so that the first time you do it, it's with me."

Ryan could not have been more surprised by her statement. He thought for sure he'd be sleeping in the cold tonight. He reflected for a moment. He'd done some pretty freaky shit. Threesome, foursomes, ass fucking, blowjobs, even some tying up and spanking here and there. But there was one thing he'd never done.

"I guess it would be true lovemaking. Man and woman holding one another, tenderly, sweetly making love to one another."

"You mean you've never…"

"Nope, always fast, freaky, or…"

"Sucking," she grinned as he nodded. She was quiet for a long time and then stood, his heart dropping, knowing that she was going to either leave or make him leave. Standing in front of him, she held out her hand. He looked confused. "Let me make love to you, Ryan, the way it should be."

Ryan slowly stood, his big hand covering hers as she pulled him toward the bedroom. Pulling back the covers, she moved to stand in front of him. Lifting the sweater over her head, she wore a pretty pink and white lace bra, her nipples already responding to the cold air. Shoving her leggings down, she was wearing a matching thong.

Ryan started to unbuckle his jeans, but she shook her head, moving his hands away. Slowly, she unhooked one button after another on his shirt, sliding her hands beneath the opening. She shoved it from his shoulders, her fingers lightly brushed his skin. Ryan thought it was the most erotic thing he'd ever experienced.

Next, her hands moved to his belt, unbuckling him. She unzipped his jeans and slid them down to reveal exactly what he'd said. He was commando. She smiled as he stepped from his jeans, her mouth trailing kisses up his big thighs until she reached his enormous cock. Keegan let out a long hot breath on his tip, her tongue flicking out to taste the precum spilling from him.

"On the bed," she said. He couldn't do anything but comply, lying back on the pillows. She lifted his jeans and raised an eyebrow. "Condom or no? I'm clean and on the pill."

"No," he growled. "I'm clean."

She nodded, her thumbs curling beneath the waistband of her thong. Wiggling those delicious hips, she let it fall, revealing a smooth, hairless pussy. Ryan moaned at the sight of her, his fist clenching and unclenching.

Crawling between his legs, Keegan kissed her way up his body, once again tasting what he was offering up. Her tongue traced the lines of his muscles, his brown nipples hard and sensitive. Trailing soft kisses up his neck to the sensitive underside of his ears and then over to his mouth, she practically inhaled him. Settling herself over his hips, he felt the heat and moisture of her body against him and moaned.

Keegan lifted her hips, gripping his thick cock. She guided his head to her opening and let herself sink slowly. He was so big she gasped, feeling him stretch her, feeling the fullness expand her beyond her dreams. Finally seated completely on him, she just sat there for a moment, her muscles contracting around him. The feeling of having Keegan bare around him was unlike anything he'd ever felt before. He might have been a man-whore, but he was a safe one and never went unwrapped.

"Fuck… Keegan…"

"Sshhh," she whispered against his lips. "Don't rush this. You're too perfect." She unhooked her bra and tossed it to the floor, her full creamy breasts now pressing against his chest.

"Baby, you're the one who's perfect."

Keegan rolled her hips in a quick snap movement, and he gasped, the feeling of her wet pussy rubbing against his body, his cock buried in her depths, molding perfectly to her body. Leaning forward, she ran her tongue along the seam of his lips, her hands delicately making butterfly touches on his skin. When he opened his mouth, she let her tongue slide in, tasting him, playing with him.

His hands moved to her hips, gripping her flesh, holding her still against him, but Keegan was having none of it. She was in control, and he would learn what lovemaking was really about. Rolling their bodies, Keegan was now safely trapped beneath him, his cock still pounding inside her. Wrapping her legs around his hips, she thrust up, and he matched her, slowly, methodically feeling the fever rise between them.

As she pulled his lips to hers, the kiss turned into something so much more. As her mouth explored his own, her nails dug into his back, the sensations causing chills to race up his spine. Her left leg came higher, hooking over one shoulder; she gripped his ass cheeks, forcing him to thrust harder and harder.

"Feel that," she said breathlessly as his body slammed into her, "feel that, Ryan. That's lovemaking, baby, not sex. You're so fucking hot, and you deserve this and so much more."

"Oh fuck, Keegan, honey..." his moans and groans were animalistic, and Keegan enjoyed every moment of it as he released inside her, filling her body with their love. As he slowed, she felt him slip from her body. Rolling to his side, he pulled her with him.

"That... was perfect," she smiled.

"Baby girl, that was better than perfect. I want to do that for the rest of our lives, Keegan." She turned quickly, staring up at him.

"Wh-what?"

"I know it's fast, honey, but I'm crazy about you, Keegan. I have never in my entire life spent more than an hour or two with any woman, none. I have spent four days with you, and it's not nearly enough. You're it for me, Keegan. If you're not there yet, that's okay. Lord knows I deserve to wait for someone as perfect as you. Just know I'm not going anywhere. I'm not leaving you, baby."

"Are you done with the speech now?" she smiled. "Good because I'm falling for you too, Ryan. I damn sure didn't want to. You were so freaking cocky and obnoxious that first night. But I still thought you were the most beautiful man I'd ever seen, and there was a sadness in you that I wanted to wipe away. I'm crazy about you, Ryan. Just please don't hurt me."

Ryan's stomach clenched. She had every right to make that statement. God knows he'd hurt more than a few women in his day. This woman, though? He'd rather cut his arm off than hurt this woman.

"Baby girl, I will never, never intentionally hurt you. Will I fuck up? Damn sure I will because I'm a stupid asshole sometimes. But I will always, always, Keegan, come back to you, honey."

"Good," she grinned.

"Now," he said, pulling her on top of him. "I think I need a few more lessons in lovemaking. Think you can help me out?"

"I can definitely help you out, Ryan O'Neal, for the rest of our lives."

CHAPTER FIFTEEN

By the second day of the blizzard, everyone was going a little cabin crazy. Grace sent a text out that they were cooking a big meal in the barn for anyone who wanted to join them. The response was an immediate, yes!

As Keegan and Ryan walked through the back door, her mother and Ty were coming down the stairs. The two brothers walked ahead to greet the other men while Keegan pulled back on her arm.

"So, how is it going?" she asked her mom.

"Keegan, if you think I'm going to tell you how my sex life is going, that's not going to happen," she grinned.

"Why? They're twins, Mom. I can pretty much guess that what Ryan has, Ty has as well, and if so, rock on, Mom!" she giggled.

"Oh my God," she blushed. "Keegan, I'm not talking about Ty's penis compared to his twin's."

"I bet they're the same," smiled Keegan. She knew she was embarrassing her mom, but she was having so much fun, and truth be told, she was thrilled that her mom was happy. Tinley simply shook her head in a vehement 'no,' she was not having this discussion.

"Well, since you're my mom, and I've always told you everything... Ryan is amazing. I mean, he's so beautiful, Mom. I look at that body and can't believe he's mine. At least, that's what he says. He's unbelievable in every way, and you may not want to say it or hear it, but my man is spectacular in bed."

Tinley looked at Ty and smiled. The way Keegan spoke about Ryan was exactly how she felt about Ty, but she just couldn't bring herself to say it to her daughter.

"Just know that I'm happy, Keegan," she finally resolved. "Ty is… he's everything I never knew I wanted or needed." Keegan grinned at her mom and nudged her shoulder.

"And he's great in the sack, right?"

"Oh, for God's sake! I'm not, no, oh, hell, yes. He's a fucking stallion in bed."

"I knew it!" yelled Keegan as the entire room turned to stare at them. Tinley blushed a fiery red, while Keegan just smiled and waved. "I knew they were the same… long… thick…" Tinley placed her hands over her ears and started singing.

"Nope, lalalalalala…" She walked toward Ty, then turned and winked, blowing a kiss toward her daughter. There were some advantages to being this close in age. Speaking about sex was probably not at the top, but it was definitely an advantage. Keegan followed her mom to the hunky brothers.

"What were you two laughing about?" asked Ryan.

"I was just telling my mom I hoped Ty was packing as much as you," she grinned. Ty nearly spit his beer across the room as Ryan let out a barking laugh. "Oh, come on. You two didn't compare notes about us? Aren't curious if mother and daughter share the same…"

"NO!" yelled Ty. "I am not discussing my woman with my brother, and I do not want to hear about whatever you have or don't have."

"Oh," she grinned, "well, that's a shame." Ryan was still laughing as they took their seat. Keegan snuggled in beside him, the heat of her skin filling his soul.

"I told you that first night," said Tinley, "no filter whatsoever." Ty hugged her to his body and nodded, kissing the top of her head. He led her further down the tables away from his brother and Keegan. He liked Keegan well enough, but he was not curious at all about what she looked like or acted like in bed with his twin.

"Hi, Tinley," said Bree. "How are you settling in?"

"Good, thank you, Bree. This place... these people are really incredible. I have to say, I was obviously pretty skeptical and scared when I first met Ty, but you all immediately put me at ease."

"I know what you mean. This is an amazing group of men and women. There are no judgments here for anyone. I know you were bothered initially about your age difference with Eagle. I mean Ty, but no one cares, honey, at all. First of all, you look so young; no one would ever know."

"But they will eventually," she grimaced.

"Maybe, maybe not, but who gives a shit. He loves you. That's plain as the nose on your face. It doesn't matter as long as you're good with it." Tinley nodded, her sable hair falling into her face. Ty turned and immediately tucked a big strand behind her ear. Bree couldn't help but smile at the sweet, romantic gesture. Looking further down the table, she noticed Ryan and Keegan laughing, his hands never leaving her body, always needing to touch, reassure that she was there.

"Seems Keegan has found her future as well," smiled Bree. Tinley nodded, grinning at the other woman.

"I think she has, which surprises me. Ty told me that everyone pretty much considered Ryan a man-whore, but I have to say, my daughter was pretty much a free spirit as well. I worried about her, but maybe she just needed someone like her to finally settle down."

"Maybe, or maybe they both needed something that the other provided," said Bree. "Hawk needed a woman to prove that she wouldn't run, and Keegan needed a man to prove he was loving and compassionate. Seems to me they both scored on that one."

Tinley smiled at the other woman, looking down the table to her daughter. Maybe that's exactly what she needed all this time. A man who wasn't going to leave her, wasn't going to hurt her or abuse her. She needed Ryan, and Ryan definitely needed her.

As the meal ended and music kicked up, the couples danced for a bit and then Amanda took the floor, giving them all a few songs to sway to. When she sang, "I Love The Way You Love Me," Ty grabbed Tinley and held her in such a delicate, sweet embrace, she thought she might weep right there on the floor. As the song ended, he knelt down in front of her and pulled out a big ring box.

"Ty..." she gasped.

"Marry me, Tinley. Marry my sorry sad ass so I won't be sad or sorry anymore. I love you, baby; I have since the moment we met. Marry me and have my babies."

"Oh, wow," she said, reaching down tentatively for the ring. The huge yellow diamond shone in the red velvet box. Her fingers gently touched the top of the stone and then looked down at Ty, his eyes filled with expectation. "Yes, yes, I'll marry you."

Placing the ring on her finger to the cheers of those around them, he swung Tinley around, kissing her. Keegan stepped up, hugged her mom, and then turned to Ty.

"Daddy," she whined, "I need a raise in my allowance."

"Fucking hell, no," he growled. "Do not... ever... call me that again. I love you, Keegan, because you're Tinley's daughter, and my idiot brother is in love with you, but I am not now, nor will I ever be your dad. How about friend?"

"W-wait..." she said, swallowing, "wait... y-you... you said 'your idiot brother'..."

"Loves you," he grinned. "Yep." Keegan turned, walking straight toward Ryan. He saw the woman marching directly toward him, and from the look on her face, he was certain he'd already fucked something up.

"Keegan, what's wrong, baby? Aren't you happy for them?"

"Y-you l-love me," she whispered. Ryan, startled, stepped back, and looked down at her, then looked over at his brother and back at her, smiling.

"Yea, baby, I love you. I've known for a few days now, but I didn't want to scare..." Her lips crashed against his, her legs wrapping around his waist.

"I love you too," she said breathlessly. "I love you too, you big idiot." Ryan laughed, gripping her ass cheeks in both hands.

"Good thing, baby. I'd hate to have to kidnap you to get you to fall in love with me," he smiled. "How do you feel about a double wedding?" Looking back at her mom, she smiled.

"I think I love that idea," she grinned.

"Good, let's go back to the cottage and ring shop while I make love to you." It would be another hour before Tinley realized her daughter was back in the cottage, ring shopping, with her fiancée.

Later that evening, lying next to Ty, her hand resting on his chest, the big ring sparkling in the light of the room. Flickers of snowflakes falling, the moonlight reflecting on them, made prisms across the room. Their naked bodies were wrapped around one another, her core wet and a little sore from three rounds of lovemaking. It took only a week. A week for her to meet, fall head over heels in love and become engaged to a man she didn't believe she deserved.

Fate has a strange way of working out for you. In her head, she wondered if her parents were even alive any longer. Her grandmother was long gone, but something inside her wanted to be able to tell her parents how wrong they were about her. She'd survived, she and her daughter both. Not only survived, but they thrived. She was successful, happy, and in love.

Curling into his side, she wrapped a leg over his waist, and he moaned, gripping her thigh and pulling it higher, his hands sliding down toward her apex of desire.

"I love you," she whispered.

"Not as much as I love you, baby girl."

CHAPTER SIXTEEN

Ace tapped on Ghost's door and heard his gravelly voice say something close to 'come in.'

"Got a minute?" he asked.

"If I said no, would it matter?" he said, staring at the younger man. Ace's face was without expression or emotion. He knew the question was rhetorical. He was just waiting for Ghost to verify. "Come in, Ace. What's up?"

"Ralph Tolbert. He's getting more help than we thought."

"Wait, we thought Dawg was the one probably getting help. Why would someone help Ralph?"

"Dawg is helping Tolbert and vice versa. Tolbert is his nephew. He most likely knew about him stealing from the club, and my guess is he is the backer for his current business. When things went to shit, Dawg left Vegas. Tolbert, however, stayed in Nevada, continuing to work their businesses. He runs what, on the surface, appears to be a legitimate escort business called Dolls by Night."

"Cute," he murmured.

"Yea, not so much. The women on the books, the ones he's actually reporting, are of age, check out, and live in and around Vegas. However, that's not what's really happening. He's kidnapping young girls, getting them hooked on the drugs, and then pimping them. The

Bastards were always drug runners, but now we know how deep it goes. His source for heroin and cocaine appears to be one Alonzo Gutierrez. The butcher of Guadalajara."

"Fuck, Ace, do you have anything good to tell me?" he moaned. Whiskey, Razor, and Eagle stepped in behind him.

"Afraid not. Gutierrez sends shipments through to him in Vegas twice a month. They arrive by charter plane, land in the desert away from prying eyes, and are then split up, hauled to other locations, sold, and the money laundered through Dolls by Night."

"Is he supplying girls to Gutierrez?" asked Whiskey.

"Not sure yet, but it would make sense. None of the girls found so far are older than sixteen, and there's a list a mile long for Nevada, Utah, Colorado, and California of missing girls in this age group. Ivan called in this morning. He's on another case but knows that they've been watching these guys. Although they don't have their full contingent from the Bastards, who they do have are the worst of the worst."

"What he was able to tell me is that the girls are taken, either willingly or unwillingly, and made to party with the guys. They give them a few hits of the drugs, and then they own them. Once they have them there, they train the girls. Take their virginity violently, and make sure they know how to do what the men want."

"What do we need to do to pull this guy, Dawg, out?" asked Eagle.

"We need to stop Brick," said Ace. "If we stop him, whatever he's doing to help Dawg stay in hiding will stop, and he'll come out, and we'll get to him. My suggestion? We need to send a few guys in, find this number to call him, and order a girl or two. If he sends someone with the girls, which we believe he's doing, get the guy and force him to tell you where they

keep the girls. If you close down his operation, he'll have nothing."

"I'm not closing him down. I'm killing him," said Eagle. "I know we need to get those

girls, but if you think I'm going to let that motherfucker walk, you've all lost your minds."

"Not gonna let him walk, Eagle," said Ghost. "Just let us get the information we need,

and he's all yours."

"Okay, I'll book five? Six tickets to Vegas for this weekend. I'm gonna call the Aces and

see if we can get some loner bikes. It'll be cold there, but you shouldn't mind riding in that."

"Ace?" said Ghost. "Thanks for everything, brother, fantastic work. Book us several

rooms at an off-the-strip hotel. We can't look like we've got money. No kuttes, no tats

showing if possible. We want to go in unseen and unidentifiable."

By the time Ace wrote down all the details of what would be needed, the room was

filled with every last man watching Ghost, waiting for instructions.

"Our number one priority is to get Brick, but I won't lie when I tell all of you, the close

number one is getting those girls out of there," he said, staring at Eagle.

"You don't have to tell me, Ghost. Our job is to rescue those girls. As long as I can get

within a mile of that prick, he'll take his last breath once I have him in my sights." Eagle was

practically spitting nails, ready to kill the man who'd hurt his woman.

"It'll be me, Whiskey, Zulu, Eagle, Hawk, and Gunner. Tango? You and Doc are in charge

while we're gone. Let the girls know that we'll be out of town but that no one is to leave this property. Tango, Doc, Razor, Skull, Ace, Ice, Axe, and George will all be here. We shouldn't have any trouble at this end since no one knows they're here."

"These are the most recent mug shots for Brick and Dawg," said Ace, clicking a button on his keyboard, fifteen phones pinged in the room. "It's unlikely they've changed at all. Not the best-looking guys in the bunch, that's for sure. Brick is probably close to fifty now. Dawg is easily seventy. I'm not sure how he could place blame on the club learning about the books on Tinley. She was long gone, ten years gone, by the time everything went down, but he may very well think it's her."

"I have a question," asked Hawk. "If we were able to find all this information, the drop spots for the drugs, the affiliation with Gutierrez, the girls, why haven't the feds dropped the hammer on this little operation?"

All eyes stared at Hawk, his moment of complete clarity without his usual rhetoric and bullshit humor was something new. After staring at Hawk for a few seconds, they turned to Ace.

"Gutierrez is in the feds pocket."

"What the fuck?" growled Ghost.

"He's helping them get to another group in Mexico who are affiliated with Isis and the Taliban."

"In Mexico?" questioned Ghost.

"Yep. It's cheap, easy to get to, easy to hide out, and there is a sympathetic ear for anyone hating Americans. Gutierrez made an agreement that he would help them if they ignored his little shipments into Nevada."

"Fuck, that means if we disrupt that shit, we're going to have the feds on us," said Whiskey.

"Not necessarily," smiled Ace. "The plane is going to have an... accident. Since the Ace's know the plane, the plane numbers, and the call letters on the plane, I can tap into their communications, screw with their onboard navigation systems, and, well, let's just say they're going to miss the proper altitude over the mountains by a few thousand feet. I'll make it happen on the shipment after you guys have left Nevada."

"Ace, you are a fucking genius," grinned Eagle. "So, their planes will go down with the drugs, which will be found by local authorities and can't be ignored. Gutierrez will be out the drugs, the plane, and any men on board."

"That's the plan," smiled the other man.

Ghost shook his head, laughing as he did. Ace was exceptional in every way, and until recently, his genius was often hidden due to his inability to manage crowds and human contact. The beautiful Charlie changed all that with him, and now he was thriving in an environment where he could not only be around people but felt freer to express his ideas.

"I'll have burners waiting for all of you the morning you leave. Try to look like weekend bikers, frat brothers reunited for a wild Vegas weekend or something. No kuttes, I might even suggest buying new boots to make it look like you're pretenders."

Whiskey nodded, looking down at his favorite boots. They were scuffed, marked up, his gear shift toe was almost completely devoid of leather, and if he were honest, they needed to be re-soled. He didn't mind buying another pair, but they were going to have to cut these ones off his feet.

"You're in luck because there's a convention next weekend. It's a concrete convention."

"Concrete?" asked Eagle.

"Yea, like the shit they pave roads with and build buildings – concrete. I'm going to send you some basic information. Read it on the plane just in case." He turned to look at his computers and knew that no one was leaving behind him. "Uh, that's all I have."

Ghost shook his head, smirking at the younger man.

"Alright, enjoy your next three days with the wives. Hopefully, this fucking snow will stop, and we can get the hell out and back on time. I'll talk to the sheriff and make sure he knows you all might call him while we're out of town. Let's go, gentlemen, no one left behind, not one fucking person."

The men filtered out of the room into the restaurant, which was still closed due the blizzard. The kids were running or crawling around, the women all huddled together talking about something. Hawk stopped inside the door, just staring at Keegan. His heart felt as though it might pound through his chest. Looking at his brother, he realized he had the same expression on his face, staring at Tinley.

"Fucking amazing, isn't it, Ty?" he said, smiling at his brother. He nodded.

"I never thought I'd be this spellbound by a woman, Ry, never."

"I know, man, me neither. I can't believe we found it in a mother-daughter duo," he laughed. "Although, I guess it makes sense with us. It was either this or twins."

"Naw, man," said Eagle. "This-this is what I was waiting for. My whole fucking world right there, Ryan. I wish dad was here to see it."

"He is, man. Believe me, he is."

CHAPTER SEVENTEEN

"So, is this one of those things where what happens in Vegas stays in Vegas?" asked Keegan that night in the cottage, eyeing him carefully from the corner of the room.

"Yes, but not in that way," he laughed. "This is about Brick and Dawg, honey. You know that. Sometimes, Keegan, sometimes we take on jobs or missions, fuck. We all still call them missions. Sometimes we take on missions and can't really tell you all the details. I'll always tell you whatever I can, but we do it for your safety and the safety of the men."

"I get it," she said, nodding. "I just, I guess I'm nervous because there's a lot of temptation in Vegas and…"

"The old me would be thrilled about going out there, baby. The new me? Not so much. I want to curl up in that bed in there and fuck you for the next fifty years. This has to be done, Keegan. I cannot rest knowing that those two men are out there ready to harm you or your mom." She fell into his open arms and nodded against his chest.

"I know, and I love you all the more for that. I'm just being an insecure little ninny. That's all."

"No, you're not. You're being a loving fiancée who is worried because her once asshole boyfriend is going to a place where naked girls are the norm. Except there's only one naked girl I want, honey, only one. I will text you or call you every morning and every night. Don't forget, my brother will be with me, watching out for me, as will the other guys."

"Can we stay in the cottage until you leave?" she asked. Ryan laughed, never before having been with a woman who wanted his company for more than a few hours or that he wanted to be around for more than a few hours.

"We can definitely stay in the cottage until we leave, baby. I want you, Keegan, all the fucking time. I'm hard for you no matter where I am, and no image of another woman is going to take that away. You are it for me, Keegan, it."

"I love you, Ryan, so deeply it's hard for me to breathe sometimes."

"I know, baby girl, me too." He kissed her again and then pulled back. "I have an idea; what do you say we create our own romantic getaway here? I'll push the furniture back. We'll pull the mattress out here in front of the fire, and we'll pretend we're camping. We've got marshmallows and hot dogs; I think we even have stuff to make s'mores. What do you say?"

"I say you're a romantic at heart, Ryan. I say, yes, that sounds perfect."

Ryan pushed the furniture to the side and cleared the living room, then carried the big king-sized mattress out in the middle of the floor, setting it in front of the fire. It seemed just as he got everything settled, the power went out. He smiled at Keegan as he put another log on the fire. They dressed in as much clothing as they could stand and then cuddled beneath the blankets, talking for hours.

As Ryan started to drift off to sleep, he felt Keegan's warm hands pushing at his clothing and grinned. Fucking awesome being woken up by the woman you love exploring your body. She was naked, sitting on his erect cock. Already moving back and forth, the firelight dancing on her skin, her thick hair swaying against the light.

Ryan reached up, squeezing her breasts, tweaking at her big nipples as she moaned his name. Pulling one hand from her breast, she took one long finger in her wet mouth, sucking it, her tongue curling around it.

"Oh, baby girl, fuck, Kee…"

"I know, I know. You're so damn hot…" He shook his head.

"You are the one, baby. You're more than I ever imagined, Keegan. You are everything to me, baby girl, everything. We're gonna be married, honey, and one day when you're ready, we're gonna have babies, lots of them." She laughed, nodding her head.

"Five," she smiled.

"Seven, two sets of twins," he grinned.

"Six with one set of twins," she said, rocking harder, rubbing her clit as he pumped into her, his fingers gripping the flesh of her breast.

"Fuck it," he growled, screaming his release, "as many as you want, baby, as many as you can carry. I love you, Kee. I love you so fucking much, baby." He held her against him, the tears welling in his eyes as he did. She inched closer, pulling the blankets over their bodies, staring at his face.

"Why are you crying? Did I do something?" she asked with a trembling lip.

"Yea, you did something. You shattered every fucking wall around my heart, baby. I had this perfect fortress built around that damn thing, and then you walked in, and it crumbled.

I can't lose you, Keegan. I think I would curl up and die if you left me." She leaned on her

elbow, her long hair brushing his shoulder, her breasts gently swaying against his chest.

"I am not going anywhere, Ryan," she said, looking down at him. "We're a mess, aren't

we? I think you're gonna fuck around on me, and you think I'm gonna leave you. Let's get this

straight. I won't leave you if you don't fuck around on me. You don't fuck around on me,

knowing I won't leave you. Clear?" Ryan laughed, wiping his eyes.

"Clear, baby. God, I love you."

"I know because I love you too, Ryan. You know, Scott, Skull is really responsible for us

getting together."

"How so, honey?"

"Well, when he offered for me to stay in his room, I think he could sense that I was only

doing it to make you jealous. When I walked by you, I was hoping you would reach out and

grab me. I don't know, throw me over your shoulder or something. By the time we got up to

his room, he knew that I wasn't into it. He was so nice about it."

"He's a fucking stellar dude," he grinned. "Spent more than fifteen years in the Coast

Guard boarding drug vessels and refugee boats mostly. Guy saw as much action as any

Marine."

"I was thinking. I might know someone."

"Nope, nope, nope," he said, shaking his head. "Rules of the house, honey. We don't fix anyone up. Let things happen. It's what happened for us and look how it turned out." She pouted but nodded her head, lying back down into the curve of his arm.

"Do you really think we might have twins?" she grinned.

"It's certainly a good chance, but I sure fucking hope so."

"Why?"

"Because I know that my twin was there for me my entire life. No one was a better friend than Ty. I always had someone to play with, always had someone to get into trouble with. I watch Zulu and Gabi's boys and think, that's us, that's me and Ty twenty-six years ago. They're gonna grow up as each other's right hand. Nothing explains the connection of a twin, and I want at least two of our babies to feel that."

Keegan nodded, her hand lightly playing against his chest. She let her fingers slide down his muscled abdomen, finding what she was seeking, the semi-hard rod waiting for her touch.

"I can't get enough of you," she whispered. Ryan rolled her quickly onto her back, his big body trapping her against the mattress, his hands suddenly everywhere at the same time.

"That's fucking awesome, baby, because I can't get enough of you either."

CHAPER EIGHTEEN

Ty stepped out of the shower, the towel wrapped around his waist. He could hear Tinley moving around in the room and smiled to himself. His fiancée was in the other room. Fucking amazing. He pulled the towel from his body and walked out to see her standing in just the tiniest fucking thong, no bra. She was fixing something on the table, and he just watched her, finally clearing his throat. She jumped, turning with a blush.

"Whatcha got, babe?" he grinned.

"Oh, ummm, a surprise. Lay down," she instructed. No way in hell was he going to say no. Last time she fucking blew his mind, so he wasn't going to be an idiot about this. "You showered. You-you might need to shower again when we're done."

He looked at her with a funny expression as she walked toward him with a bowl. Lifting the spoon, he knew immediately what it was, chocolate sauce. Sticking her pinky in the bowl, she pulled it out, the long trail of chocolate falling to the bowl as she brought her finger to her lips, licking the liquid from her hand. Ty was already painfully hard watching her.

Taking the spoon, she lifted it once more, drizzling the warm sauce over the top of his dick. When she was satisfied with the amount, she lowered her mouth to him, wrapping that beautiful pink tongue around his cock, licking and sucking.

"Ohhhh, fuck," he moaned. Standing once more, grabbing a canister from the tray, she smiled at him, squirting whipped cream around her sensitive nipples.

"I need you to lick this off of me, Ty. Do a very, very good job, and I have another surprise for you." He nodded, unable to speak as she sat beside him, his mouth covering the first breast, licking every drop of the sweet cream from her tits. Then he started on the second one, lapping it up, her body arching into his mouth. When he was done, she scooted away from him, his cock pulsing with need.

Tinley returned with a jar of honey, placed a small bit over his nipples, and went to work. When she was done, his nipples were so raw and sensitive, he wasn't sure he would ever be able to wear a shirt again.

"Are you ready for your surprise, Ty?" He couldn't speak, just nodded. "I want to hear you say it, honey." Her voice was like velvet, sliding over his body.

"Y-yes, yes, I want my surprise," he said. Tinley pushed the thong down and then turned, bending over for him to see the big pink butt plug firmly planted in her ass. "Holy fucking shit."

"It feels so full, honey. I've been wearing it all day for you. I want you to take it out and put you in. Will you do that for me?" she asked.

"Fucking hell, yes, I will. Come here, baby," he rumbled. Tinley placed her knees on the edge of the bed and bent over, her perfect round ass poking straight up at him. Ty gripped the plug, turning it gently.

"Ohhhh, wow, baby, that feels… it feels so good…" she moaned. Shit! He was never going to last the night with this. Turning the plug again, he gently released it, her tight hole now winking at him. Reaching into the nightstand, he pulled out a tube of lubricant, slathering his cock, groaning from his own touch.

"Oh," she said, jumping up, "one more thing." One more thing? What the fuck was this woman doing to him? From the tray, she lifted a small purple vibrator. "Once you're in my backside, this will go in my front."

"Tinley, precious girl, you're sure?" She nodded, nibbling on her lip as she bent over again. Ty let the head of his big cock touch her hole, and he almost exploded against her ass. Biting back a curse, he inched forward. "You good, baby?"

"Y-yes, you're so big, but it feels so good." Shit! He moved further in, his big head all the way inside her, gently moving back and forth, a little more of his cock entering each time. When he was fully seated inside her, he held his breath, waiting for her to say something.

"Wow, that's so, I feel so full, but it's amazing. Damn, you feel so good, Ty."

"Me? Woman, you fucking break me! I gotta move, baby girl." She nodded, lifting the vibrator to her clit. The second she flicked it on, he felt the vibrations to his core. She was going to blow any second with the feeling of him fucking her ass and the little vibrator working her clit.

"Ty, now, baby, now. Cum in my ass!" she yelled. He happily obliged, his load spilling inside her, coating his cock as it thrust in and out, her own orgasm spasming through her body. Tinley looked over her shoulder, her face flush with desire and a bit of embarrassment at her brazenness.

"Was it good? Did I do okay?" she asked. Ty pulled out of her ass, feeling himself already hardening again. He flipped her around and lifted her against his body, walking back to the shower.

"Good? That was fucking out of this world, Tinley. You amaze me every damn day, baby, every damn day. I love your body, honey, every fucking inch of it, and I will always do anything you want to do as long as it doesn't hurt you. I love you, honey, so much," he said, setting her down inside the shower.

Tinley smiled, happy that she'd made him happy. She wasn't sure how she would feel about anal sex, but the books by Charlie made it sound really erotic and, if done right, enjoyable. Ty definitely did it right. Using the butt plug was smart on her part, but with his thick, long cock she was worried about it hurting. No doubt her ass would be sore tomorrow, but for now, she was sated.

After showering for a second time, Ty and Tinley crawled between the sheets just as the power went out. He smiled down at her as light filtered in from the window, the flakes dancing across the room once more.

"Can I ask you something?" she said quietly.

"Baby girl, you're mine. You can ask me any damn thing you want," he grinned.

"D-do you make enough, I mean, is your salary enough that I could maybe not work so much when we have kids?" she asked. Ty pulled her into his body more tightly, smiling as he did. Fuck yea, she was thinking about their babies.

"Honey, you can stay home all you want. I make good money, Tinley, really good. We'll build a house here, and if you want, you can take part-time work from home, but you won't need to."

"I'm so glad to hear that. I worked all the time with Keegan and didn't really get a chance to enjoy her childhood with her. If…"

"When…"

"When we have children, I want to be able to give them that. I want to be the kind of mom you'll be proud of," she whispered. Laying her flat on her back, Ty leaned over her, staring into her eyes.

"Listen to me, baby girl. You are a fucking amazing mother. No one better. Our kids are gonna be blessed to have you as their momma. You will be the hot mom in the carpool line, and I will be the young dad that keeps up with his kids. Couples are gonna be so jealous of us," he smiled. Tinley laughed, a tear slipping from her eyes.

"You are everything I will ever need, baby girl, and our babies will have an amazing upbringing with two parents who love them and love each other. If you want to do some work from home, maybe we talk to Ghost about you handling the books for our business."

"Really?" she asked excitedly.

"Really, baby, once everything is settled, we'll talk to him." She kissed him passionately, their bodies nearly fusing together. "You tired, honey?"

"I'm not," she grinned, "what did you have in mind?"

"Still some whipped cream left over, and I have an active imagination."

CHAPTER NINETEEN

By Friday, they were saying their goodbyes and waving as the guys made their way to the airport. At curbside, it was a bit like watching a clown car unload, legs and arms stretched out of the SUV, all the men over six-feet, all over two hundred pounds of muscle.

It wasn't much different during boarding. Six huge men boarding a plane, dressed in jeans, motorcycle boots, covered in tattoos, and most sporting beards, was definitely something to make the passengers squirm. They occupied the exit rows and promptly fell asleep, not waking until they felt the descent of the plane. It was something they'd all learned to do in the service. Sleep when you can, you may never get another opportunity.

Although Vegas was cold, there was no snow, and they were eternally grateful for that. Waiting in baggage claim was Knuckles with three of his men.

"Ghost, you old fuck," he said, pulling him for a hug "Semper Fi, bitch."

"Fuck you, asshole. If you wanna kiss Marines, kiss Gunner, Whiskey, and the billboard twins."

"Gunner, Whiskey, good to see you boys looking as ripped as ever. You two were Marines as well?" he asked.

"Yes, sir, MARSOC snipers." Ryan stood tall and straight, no smirks, no smartass comments, and Ghost could only grin at the younger man.

"Well, you're sure as shit built like Marines. Zulu, you still got that thyroid problem, buddy?" he smirked, looking up at the man, his six-foot-six height towering over his own six-feet even.

"Fuck off, asshat. I got a beautiful wife who feeds me well."

"No shit? Someone actually married your huge ass?" Zulu grinned but flipped him the middle finger. "Let's go. My boys are outside with a trailer with six bikes on them. Sure like 'em back the way I'm givin' 'em to you, Ghost."

"Don't worry, man, anything happens, we'll replace it with one of our own, my word." They walked out to the curbside pickup and down along the curve of the sidewalk. Walking further toward the offsite parking, a huge truck stood with a trailer attached and six gleaming motorcycles behind it.

"Pick your weapon," said Knuckles. "My boys will get it off for you. Where you fellas stayin'?"

"We're at the Desert Roadside Inn," said Whiskey. Knuckles nodded as he signaled his men to remove the bikes.

"Good, it's on the outskirts, decent, but not overly so. You won't have to fight roaches, but don't expect room service. Two more girls went missing this week. My boys have been chasing down leads, but they're always the same with this guy. We're pretty sure he scopes the girls out at the mall, school, even their social media pages."

Eagle and Hawk both looked at one another. If he was scouring social media pages, he could have come across the photos of Keegan and Tinley.

"I'm tellin' ya, Ghost, this fucker is sick. The way these girls are left – ripped apart from the inside out and their poor bodies. I almost hate bringin' them back to their parents."

"I know, man, I know. But it's why we do this shit, right? Get the filth off the street and fight another day. I got a son of my own now and another on the way. Whiskey's wife is pregnant. Gunner has a little girl, and Zulu has twin boys. We're all doing this for our kids, man." The older man nodded and watched as each man grabbed a bike he was comfortable with.

"Here's the number for the service. Just tell them you're looking for someone, young, innocent, and who doesn't mind a little pain," he ground out between his teeth. "According to everything we know, a fucker will show up with a girl and collect the money. You get twelve hours with her, which you won't need. If you need us, me or my boys, you call, Ghost. None of us were spec ops, but most of us served, and we can damn sure wield a weapon. Don't go into this war alone."

"Appreciate it more than you know, Knuckles," he said, gripping the man's hand. "We're gonna grab some food, hit the hotel, and take a drive to the other place to see what's goin' on." The old man nodded again, waving as they pulled away.

"Who were they, Knuckles?" asked his man, ron.

"Fucking heroes, brother. Biggest group of fucking heroes I've ever met, and I'm damn proud to know 'em. Let's keep our ears peeled for 'em. I want them all goin' home to their families."

"You got it, boss," said Iron, walking back toward the truck.

"For once, just once, someone, please watch over those boys," he whispered.

CHAPTER TWENTY

The hotel was pretty much as Knuckles said it would be. The rooms were clean, although the carpet could use replacing. Most of the men didn't care as long as the beds were decent with clean sheets. They paired off, two to a room, and then walked across the parking lot to a diner.

Sitting at the only six-person booth, the men squeezed in as a middle-aged woman walked over to take their order.

"So, let me repeat," she said with an eyebrow raised. "Four double cheeseburgers, six orders of fries, two orders of onion rings, three sirloins, two stacks of pancakes, one chocolate milkshake, two strawberry, and four vanilla, two BLTs, and six slices of apple pie, when you're done. Is that right?"

"Don't forget the ice cream on the pie," said Hawk.

"You boys wanna share the secret of eating all that and still lookin' like you do?" she grinned.

"Just good genetics, ma'am," smiled Eagle.

"Whatever, sugar. I'll be right back with your drink orders." The guys looked around at the crowd, mostly men wearing tags from the conventions in town. Two young girls, probably in high school, walked through the front doors and sat at the counter. Their jeans were so tight, they slid down their backsides, revealing an unhealthy amount of skin.

Ghost looked at the others and frowned.

"I will ground Calla for life if she ever wears something like that," said Gunner under his breath. Eagle nodded but wasn't really paying attention. What he was paying attention to was the man standing in the parking lot, watching the girls through the window.

"I think the girls are being watched," said Eagle. All eyes looked at him, staring straight in his direction. "Man outside near the bus stop, but he's looking straight through the window at the girls."

"Think he's part of the group we're looking for?" asked Hawk.

"Don't know, but we should warn those girls to go home," he said.

"And we look like the creepy old guys," said Zulu, frowning. He stood and walked toward his waitress, whispering to her as she nodded, her face filled with fear. He stepped back to his table and watched as she moved toward the two young girls, speaking softly. The girls nodded and followed the woman toward the back of the restaurant. A few minutes later, she came back to the table.

"Dinner's on me," she said, grinning.

"You don't have to do that," said Zulu.

"I do. Got two girls of my own, grown, but still. Them girls were prime targets paying more attention to their damn phones than what was around them. I got 'em out the back and through the laundromat on the back side. They called their parents to pick 'em up. Good job, boys." She smiled as she walked away, and Eagle continued to watch the man. Not seeing the girls, he got frustrated, pacing back and forth, and finally headed back to his car, burning rubber as he pulled out of the parking lot.

"Piece of shit," growled Gunner.

The table was covered with plates of food, forcing their waitress to set some of them on the adjacent table. By the time they were done eating, every plate was clean, and the guys weren't even all that full.

"Let's go. I wanna ride by the motel where this shit takes place."

Traveling at night on the bikes was smarter than during the day. No one would see their faces or think twice about motorcyclists passing through this part of Vegas. Driving to the far outskirts of the city, they found the address and parked across the street at an old filling station, pretending to check the air in their tires.

All of the men took note of two men standing outside two separate rooms at the small motel across the street, both smoking and bullshitting with one another. Hawk looked at his brother and nodded as he moved around the bikes and the pumps, casually walking down the side of the motel and to the back side. As he approached the windows, he heard the telltale grunting and groaning of people having sex, although it sounded like mostly male voices.

At the second window, he stopped, listening intently, when he heard the voices of two men.

"Fuck her ass while I take her pussy," he told his friend. "Sweet little young thing, aren't you?"

Shit! Muttered Hawk. He wanted to save that girl, but if he did anything stupid, there would be hell to pay in trying to find their guy tomorrow. Looking at the old building, he finally had an idea, praying that everything was in working order. Stepping into the breezeway, he covered his elbow and cracked the glass, pulling on the old fire alarm. Sure enough, the sirens blared. He heard the men outside the rooms pounding on the doors.

"Pull it up. Gotta go," they hollered. Hawk made his way casually across the street to the grinning faces of his brothers, including his twin.

"One room had two men," he said, nodding toward the two guys coming out of the room. The young girl was barely dressed in a cream-colored slip dress. She had to be freezing in the night air, but dickhead number one just shoved her into his truck and took off. The second door opened, and an old man, probably weighing in at almost three hundred pounds, stepped out, barely able to get his buckle done.

The other man was screaming at him as he took off toward his car. Stepping into the room, they could see shadows moving around the motel room, and then the man reappeared with a girl flung over his shoulder, barely looking alive.

"Fuck," muttered Ghost.

"You did good, Hawk," said Gunner.

"I couldn't listen to it. I wanted to break down the doors, but I knew we couldn't," he said, shaking his head.

"Let's go," said Ghost. "We need sleep, and then tomorrow, we're gonna call this prick and then kill him."

CHAPTER TWENTY-ONE

"How do you think the guys are doing?" asked Keegan to the room full of women.

"Sweetie," said Grace, smiling, "you're going to have to learn to be patient. They've only been gone two days, and sometimes they're gone for a week or more on these trips." Keegan grimaced and nodded her head.

"It's all for good reason," said Darby. "These men are truly amazing. They spent a lifetime protecting our freedom and our rights on foreign and domestic soil, then when they retire, they decide they're not quite done yet and form the Steel Patriots, rescuing trafficked and abused women, stopping drug runners, and more. That's pretty amazing to me."

"I know. Really, I do. I guess I'm just worried." Keegan looked at her mom, who gave her a sympathetic smile.

Razor and Tango walked in the room wearing their coveralls splattered with grease and paint. Tinley inwardly grinned at how handsome they were, even all dirty and without wearing anything flattering to enhance those rocking bodies.

"Hi, ladies, everyone doing okay?" asked Tango.

"We're good, honey," said Taylor, kissing her husband as he rubbed her little belly. "Keegan was just feeling a bit worried about the boys. We were trying to tell her that everything is fine."

"It's all good, Keegan, I promise. I don't know if Hawk told you, but we were all part of Special Forces in the military. That means we were training more, better, and often. We are a mixed bag of teams. Ghost, Zulu, and I were all Navy SEALs. Doc was an Army Ranger. Whiskey, Gunner, Hawk, and Eagle were all MARSOC snipers. Skull was in the Coast Guard boarding ships to search for drugs and refugees escaping their countries. Razor was part of the submarine command supporting Special Forces. Ace was Navy intelligence supporting spec ops."

"Wow, I guess I just had no idea about the history of everyone. I mean, Ryan said he was a Marine, but that's all." Tango nodded with a chuckle.

"Well, I think that says a lot about how much he's matured around you. The old Hawk would have bragged to anyone within earshot of what an amazing sniper he was. You've had a good effect on him, Keegan."

"Thank you," she smiled, "but he's had a good effect on me as well. I'm sure my mom would attest to that."

"Oh, no, no, no, you're not dragging me into this. You're my daughter, and I love you just the way you are. I do think he's good for you, and I think you're good for him. That's all I'm going to say about it."

"You're not left out of this, Tinley," said Razor. "Eagle was a broody, moody, quiet guy who pretty much spent his life keeping his brother out of trouble. He would follow him, sometimes unwillingly, to make sure he didn't get hurt. Since you've been here, he's more open, seems mellowed a bit. In our minds, those are all positive changes. I do believe all of you ladies have changed us."

"That's so sweet of you," said Tinley. "I have to confess, I'm still not completely over the age difference, but Ty keeps saying it doesn't matter to him.'

"It doesn't, sweet Tinley," smiled Tango. "That man is in love, and no amount of age difference will change that. When he left, he asked Razor and I to make sure you were safe. Said he'd die if something happened to you."

"Oh, God," she whispered, a tear sliding down her cheek.

"He loves you, honey," said Grace, smiling at the other woman. "You know, I'm not sure if you ladies know, but we all have stories about how we ended up here. Maybe, maybe if Bree has some time this week, we do a chat circle. You know, just the group of us talking about our lives and loves, our futures. I think it's a way we can understand one another a little better and maybe feel better about any insecurities we might be having."

"Insecurities? What insecurities could any of you have?" said Keegan. "You're all drop-dead gorgeous in the most beautiful of ways. You're all incredibly talented and intelligent. I see nothing to be insecure about."

"Honey, everyone feels insecure," said Gabi. "I've spent my life trying to hide my unusual looks from the world. Then that big beast of a man, the love of my life, Quin, Zulu, wraps me up and lets me know that I am perfect just the way I am."

"Same," said Bree, smiling. "I mean, I'm almost six-foot tall, exceptionally curvy, all this flaming hair, and Doc, good lord, that tall drink of water is..." She fanned herself, grinning at the other girls as they laughed.

"On that note," said Razor, "I'm going back to work. See you tonight, baby." He kissed Bella as he headed out the door, Tango on his heels after kissing Taylor.

"They're such good men," whispered Keegan.

"They are, honey, and we're good women," smiled Darby. Tinley smiled at the room of women, nodding. She looked at Grace, her small belly starting to show.

"You want to know how I feel about being pregnant at my age, don't you?" smiled Grace.

"I guess so," laughed Tinley. "I mean, I know that women are having babies later in life, but I'm so conflicted. I mean, I had Keegan so young, unexpectedly, and I've loved growing up with her. But now, to have another baby at my age, a brother or sister for Tinley who will most likely be twenty-three years old when he or she is born, it's just a bit overwhelming."

"I know, honey, but women are having babies safely, later and later in life. My pregnancy with JT was easy, and this one, so far, knock on wood, is easy as well."

"I know you're right. The thing is, I do want to have children with Ty. I mean, I'm so glad that I had Keegan, but I didn't get to share those moments with someone I loved. I love Ty so, so much, and I want to share this pregnancy with him." Gabi and Taylor smiled at the woman.

"Sounds like you made up your mind," said Gabi.

"Well, if you want my opinion," said George. The room full of women gasped, grabbing their chests in surprise.

"Shit! George, when did you get here?" asked Kat.

"Little girl, this here is my kitchen! You park your cute little butts here, and I'm gonna be right next to you whether you like it or not. Now, you didn't ask for my opinion, but I'm gonna give it cuz I know a thing or two about loving and losing."

It was as if an oracle was speaking. All the women scooted their seats closer to George, waiting to hear the wisdom he dropped on them.

"Love ain't somethin' that has an age attached to it, honey. It ain't a specific color; it don't go to a specific church. Love comes at you when you least expect it. You suddenly turn around," he said, taking Mary's hand, kissing her fingers, "and the most perfect person in the world is smiling at you.

"Now, I was a lucky man to find love twice. Lost it the first time cuz of cancer. This go-around, ain't gonna lose it. Me and Mary, we're gonna stay healthy, take our daily walks, visit beautiful Gabi as often as needed, and we're gonna take care of one another. Just like all of you will do with your men.

"Those men of yours, they're the kind of men that would rather die than hurt you or see you in pain. If there is a way to give you what you want or need, they're gonna do it. When it comes to your safety, well, ladies, just buckle up cuz ain't nothin' happenin' to any of you on their watch." George walked closer to Tinley, touching her cheek with his big rough hand and smiling down at her.

"Don't question the love right in front of you, honey. Everything, and I do mean everything, will work out. Besides, you're so beautiful you'll always look younger than that fool." The girls all chuckled, a few wiping the hormonal tears in their eyes.

"Oh, George," said Grace, rising to kiss his cheek, "you're such a good man, and you're an amazing grandfather to our babies."

"My pleasure, ladies, now get outta my kitchen. I got lunch to prepare."

CHAPTER TWENTY-TWO

"We ready?" asked Ghost, looking at Whiskey and the others. They all nodded as he dialed the number given to him. He tried to raise his voice an octave or two, not wanting to sound quite so assertive or rough.

"Dolls," said the man on the other end of the line.

"Yea, I got your number from a buddy. We're both at the convention. I was just hoping to get a girl sent over, young, maybe willing to be a little rough, nothing too bad," he said.

"We can do that," he laughed on the other end of the line. "Twelve hours costs you six hundred dollars cash. My man will bring her to you. Stay outside the door to make sure you don't damage the merchandise. You can have as many as three men on her, but no more, gotta save her for someone else next time."

Ghost nearly lost his shit, gripping the phone so hard he heard the cracking of the frame. This piece of garbage was willing to put three full-grown men on some girl who probably wasn't even eighteen.

"Yea, no problem. I'll see if one of my buddies wants a piece of her. Where do I go?" he asked. The man gave him the address of the motel and hung up.

"Let's rent a car. He'd be suspicious if we pull up on the bikes. You guys hide the bikes behind the motel. I'll make sure the girl is okay and then text you. Once we have him, we get the girl to safety, and we have twelve hours to find this son-of-a-bitch. Let's go."

Zulu rented a mid-size sedan, something very typical that a businessman would rent, while Ghost changed his clothes, pulling on a pair of Khakis, a button-up shirt, combing his hair in what he described as hipster. Hawk laughed at him as he stood there.

"You look ridiculous," he smiled.

"I feel like a fucking banker," he growled.

"Bankers don't have tattoos all over their bodies. You may need to button one more button at your neck so they don't see the tats. Fuck," growled Whiskey, "where the hell did you get those shoes? At a geriatric convention?"

"Fuck off! I didn't have a lot of choices in my shoe size, and I damn sure didn't want to spend a fortune on them."

"Alright," said Eagle, "get into the room. We'll be watching and waiting."

Ghost nodded, stepping inside the room he was told to wait. The place was disgusting. Even if he were hard up for a woman, he'd damn sure not touch anything in this place. The carpet was filthy, the bedspreads had moth holes, the television was from the 1980s, the countertops in the bathroom had cigarette burns, and the smell of mildew was prevalent.

He heard the rap of knuckles on the door, looked out to see a man gripping the arm of a young woman barely able to stand. Opening the door, he wanted to knock the asshole out.

"You order the girl?" he asked.

"Yea, hey, is she okay? She looks sick or something," he said meekly.

"Nah, she's fine, aren't you, sweetheart?" he said, slapping her ass. The girl yelped but nodded as he shoved her into the room. "Cash up front." Ghost handed the man the cash and gently took the girl's arm, pulling her into the room.

"You got twelve hours. Use her up good," he laughed. Ghost closed the door and gently set the girl on the bed. She started to lift the lightweight cotton dress over her head, and he gripped her wrists.

"No, honey, we're not doing that." She reached for his belt buckle, and he shook his head again. "Not that either. Are you okay? Are you hurt anywhere?"

Her eyes rose to meet his gaze, their grayish-blue color lifeless, the drugs obviously taking over her body. He pushed her sleeves up to see the needle marks and cursed under his breath.

"Are you hurt?" he asked again. She gave a slight shake of her head. "What's your name, honey?"

"Candy."

"What's your real name?" he asked again.

"L-Lindsey, why are you..." He held a finger to his lips and tried to see if there were any marks or injuries on her body that needed immediate attention.

"Okay, Lindsey, listen carefully. I'm not going to hurt you; I'm not going to touch you, okay. I want to help you. Where are they keeping all of you?"

"I-I don't know. They don't let us see the house. We're in a basement, and when they take us out, they put a hood over our heads. It's far, I think, because it takes us at least thirty minutes to get here."

"How many of you does he have?"

"Thirty or so," she said. Fuck! Thirty girls shoved in a basement. That had to be a good-sized basement. "W-who are you?"

"I'm someone who is going to help you get home. If you don't have a home, we'll find one for you. How old are you, honey?""

"Eighteen," she said quickly. Ghost eyed the young woman, giving her a stern look. "Fifteen."

"Fifteen," he growled. "What are they shooting you with?"

"I'm not sure. They started the minute they took me. This guy, he said he wanted to take me to a party, bought me this dress and everything. Next thing I knew, h-he stuck a needle in me, said I wouldn't feel anything this way. I opened my eyes, and there were men around me, all naked. Th-they touched me. Th-they..."

"I know, sweet girl, I know. Hold on for me, okay? You go into the bathroom, and I want you to hunker down in the tub. Don't come out until I tell you."

She nodded and headed into the bathroom. She gripped one of the threadbare towels and wrapped it around her shoulders. Ghost texted the other men, then unbuckled his pants, pulling his shirt halfway out. Opening the door, he looked up and down for the man who brought the girl.

"Hey, hey, I think there's something wrong with her. She's sick," he said, panicked.

"Fuck, you white collar boys don't get it, do you?" he said, stepping inside the room. Ghost waited until he turned, his fist connecting hard with his jaw. The man fell back on the bed, stunned. "What the fuck do you think you're coing?"

"I'm taking out the trash motherfucker," he growled as Zulu, Whiskey, Eagle, Hawk, and Gunner stepped inside.

"Oh, you assholes are gonna die," he grinned.

"Don't think so," said Eagle, pulling his weapon, the silencer secured to the end. As he did so, the others did as well, leaving the tough guy on the bed stunned.

"Wh-what do you want?"

"Where does he keep the girls?" asked Ghost, buckling his pants. He pulled off the button-up shirt, his black t-shirt now at least making him feel more comfortable and definitely giving the asshole on the bed a good view of his muscle-bound upper body.

"No fucking way, asshole. He'll kill me."

"Jesus," said Hawk, "why do these assholes always say that. You do understand that if he doesn't kill you, we will, right? You get that, don't you, genius?" Hawk stepped forward, pressing the end of the weapon against the man's groin.

"Where are the girls?" repeated Eagle.

"Henderson. He keeps them in a basement in Henderson. They're all fucked up, man. All of them. Hooked on either heroin or coke, but he barely feeds them. Most have been used so much they can barely walk."

"You helped this fucking asshole do this shit?" yelled Zulu.

"Hey, he's not exactly someone you can just say no to. Brick still has solid connections, man. Him and Dawg still plan everything out, everything. Tack on that he's getting the drugs from Gutierrez, and none of us can make a move against him."

"Yes, you can. You could if you had a set of balls," growled Gunner. "You kidnap, rape, and sell little girls. If you think that's gonna earn you any favors from us, you're fucked in the head."

"Is he at the house now?" asked Ghost.

"Never leaves. He's a paranoid fucker. Only goes out to meet Gutierrez and Dawg for the drug pickups. Those only happen twice a month, and they were just delivered yesterday. House is full of coke and heroin right now."

"Is it guarded?" asked Hawk. The man nodded.

"Six men always on the outside. Four on the inside. Two in the basement to keep the girls in-line."

"In-line?" growled Whiskey. The man couldn't even look him in the eye. Taking his keys, phone, and the small knife he carried, they searched him for other weapons, not finding anything. "End him. Wrap him in the bedspread and put him in the trunk of the rental. Leave it in the parking lot."

"The rental?" questioned Eagle.

"It's in the name of Ralph Tolbert," grinned Ghost.

"Shit, please, you don't have to kill me. You don't..." *Thwap*. The starburst pattern in his forehead silenced the room. Wrapping the man in the blanket, Zulu carried him out and tossed him in the trunk. Returning, he found Ghost calling Knuckles.

"Yea, brother, we need someone to come and pick up a little girl at the motel, yea, that motel. I may need a few vans to transport girls in a few hours. You got some boys you can spare to help us?"

"Fuck yea!" hollered Knuckles through the phone.

Ghost walked into the bathroom to see the girl in the tub, now looking much more like a little girl curled up, shaking probably from cold and the withdrawals of the drugs. He knelt down and lifted her, gently laying her on the bed. She looked up, fear in her eyes, seeing the six men.

"We're not gonna hurt you, angel, I promise. I told you, we're gonna get you home." Tears fell down her face, and she nodded, curling her legs up to her chest. They heard the rumbling of pipes and opened the door to see Knuckles with six guys on bikes, six in vans, and another in a small SUV.

"Knuckles, we got a little girl who needs help," said Ghost, taking him inside. "Lindsey, this is our friend Knuckles. He's gonna get you to a hospital, honey." She nodded, shaking violently.

Knuckles turned and called for a young man named Bear, his huge body looking very much like a big furry bear.

"Bear, take this sweet little girl to the hospital. Let them know we rescued her from a child abductor, trafficker, and drug dealer. She's probably pumped with heroin. When was your last hit, honey?" he asked.

"I-I'm not s-sure. M-maybe th-three hours."

"Shit, if she's needing every three hours, they're dosing her big," he murmured. "Bear, get her some help. She doesn't look like the one we've been searching for, but that doesn't mean anything." He nodded, leaning forward to pick up the girl as if she weighed nothing, and she didn't.

"Come on, sweet girl. Let's get you well." He turned to look at Knuckles and Ghost, lifting the girl slightly up and down. "Doesn't weigh more than eighty or ninety pounds."

Gunner and Whiskey watched as he carried the little girl to the waiting vehicle, then backed out of sight. Eagle and Hawk were already checking their weapons, readying the sniper rifles.

"You need more weapons?" asked Knuckles.

"Nope. Carried these legally here. We like our own. But damn sure can use your boys,"

he said. Knuckles nodded, waving over the rest of h s men. "Here's the plan."

CHAPTER TWENTY-THREE

"Hey, Grace, do you have a few minutes?" asked Tinley, walking toward the other woman. She was seated at one of the big round tables in the restaurant, her feet propped up on a chair, her hand lightly smoothing over her tiny belly.

"Of course, come on over," she waved, looking up at the other woman and smiling.

"Well, I don't know if I need to wait for Ghost to return, but he asked me to take a look at the books for all the businesses."

"Right, he said he was going to see if you could find any discrepancies."

"No real discrepancies, just that I think there are a whole bunch of things we could save some money on here."

"Okay, I'm listening," she said, scooting to the edge of her seat.

"Well, for instance, the beer delivery. The guy seems to just deliver the same thing every month, a mix of bottles and kegs, yet he's been charging more for delivery, upping his prices every few months. I think it was so slight, Ghost probably didn't notice, but it adds up. Also, this guy is located four towns over. There's a family-owned delivery service in the valley that would deliver for half the price."

"Holy cow, Tinley! That's amazing. I know he'll want to switch."

"Well, that's not all. The liquor guy is sending sub-premium liquor at premium pricing. He's also sending a smaller bottle when we could definitely use the bigger bottles of whiskey and bourbon. There seems to be half the amount of vodka or gin being drank, which means he can cut back on them.

"The other thing is he's sending cups, napkins, and stirrers, saying he's comping those, except he's not. It's hidden in the invoice, but he's charging for it. It's actually a lot of money over the course of a year, probably four or five thousand dollars."

"Oh wow!"

"Yea, then there's the food delivery. I know that we use some pre-made foods like the pizza crusts, bread, that sort of thing, but the vendor is slighting us on deliveries. George said he came yesterday, and according to the invoice, there should have been one-hundred-twenty-five frozen crusts, but there were only eighty. Again, I know a vendor that's closer and won't charge what this guy is charging.

"I also spoke to George and think that once spring gets here, we could plant a small garden, and we'll have fresh vegetables and herbs. I'm sure we could all lend a hand at taking care of it, and George thinks it would be something Mary would really love to take charge of."

"I can't believe you found all this, Tinley. It's amazing! I mean, you've only looked at a few things, and you've already found thousands of dollars in savings for us."

"Well, it's kind of what I do," she grinned. "I don't know as much about the garage, but I'm going to go down there in the next day or two and have a conversation with the guys about their vendors. I know that quality is seriously important to them, but some of the pieces seem ridiculously expensive."

"Yea, I have no clue what any of this is," said Grace, looking at the invoice. "I'm going to guess that Gunner, Tango, Razor, and Skull would be the guys to speak with. Maybe set up a meeting with them for when the shop is closed."

"The other thing Ghost should think about is changing the tax status for the property to a business tax. I mean, I realize that there are homes here as well, but the businesses would create a serious tax break, especially considering the work that the Steel Patriots do would qualify them as a non-profit."

"I don't think they ever thought of that. I bet Kat could tell us about filing for that status. I mean, if that side of the business was a non-profit, then maybe the guys wouldn't think twice about accepting donations or doing fundraisers. I mean, I know that they spend a lot of their own money on some of these rescue missions and that just seems a shame."

"The question for them will be how much public knowledge they want for the organization. These guys like to operate under the radar, as you well know."

"I do, or at least, I'm starting to recognize that," said Tinley. "How are you feeling?"

"Good, really good. I'm pretty sure this is going to be another boy, which seems right since my twins were girls," she smiled.

"I'm so sorry to hear about that, Grace. It must have been awful for you."

"It was, but did you know that JT is named after Eagle? I mean, Ty." Tinley shook her head. "When I arrived at those front gates, he was on gate duty. I walked up so beaten and sore I could barely breathe. He called Doc and Ghost immediately and then cradled me in his arms, so sweetly, so gently. He leaned over and said, 'You're gonna be okay. No one is gonna hurt you because only good men live here. Good men wouldn't hurt you.' It was the sweetest and most perfect thing to say."

"Oh wow," she sniffed, wiping her eyes. "He's such an amazing man. I know that. You know, part of me is pissed that I'm even questioning our age If it was reversed and he was thirteen years older than me, no one would think twice about it. There are so many stereotypes that are attached to women in relationships. I mean, no one questioned Hawk and his whoring ways, but because Keegan liked to play the field, people thought poorly of her."

"I can assure you I do not," said Grace. "I wish I would have played the field more. Maybe I wouldn't have married my insane ex-husband. I pray every day that this new generation of young women doesn't have to put up with this archaic, puritanical bullshit!"

"Amen!" said Tinley.

"Is church happening?" asked Bree and Gabi, walking in the door.

"No, we were just bitching about the double-standard for men and women in relationships," said Grace. "How was the clinic today? Busy?"

"Steady," said Gabi. "Lots of colds and flu going around. That girl, Valerie, came in with a cold. She wanted me to get Hawk for her, and I refused. She got pretty snarky when I told her he was out of town with his fiancée."

"Oh, Gabi," snickered Tinley, "you didn't?"

"Did too. I hate women like that who think they can just stake a claim on a man because they've slept with him a time or two. Hell, I don't even think Hawk slept with her. Plus, if you believe what everyone else says, the woman likes other women more than men."

"Man, he really did suck at picking women," laughed Tinley.

"I think his mother leaving them affected him far more than it did Ty for some reason," said Gabi.

"Just because they're twins doesn't mean they share everything," said Bree. "I think Hawk saw it as a betrayal, and Eagle just saw it as her leaving his father, not them. You know, I've often wondered what would make her just leave like that. I'm curious if either has ever tried to find her."

"I don't know. We could ask Ace. I mean, maybe she's out there and wants to see them." Tinley looked at the other women for guidance, but it was Bree that spoke up again.

"I don't know. I think that's really taking a step we don't want to do without their approval."

"You're right. I know that I wouldn't want Ty trying to find my parents without asking me. I'm certain my grandmother is gone by now, but as mean and stubborn as they were, I bet my folks are still alive and kicking." Kat and Taylor walked in, both rubbing their small bellies, making Tinley smile.

"Okay, ladies," said Taylor, "I think it's a share a cheesecake kind of day."

"Oh yes! I'm in," said Grace.

"Me too," said Bree.

"Done!" said Tinley. Gabi stood and stared at the women with a serious expression.

"Ladies, as your physician, I have to say I'm terribly disappointed in you. As your friend, I'll race you to the kitchen."

CHAPTER TWENTY-FOUR

The house was located on the outskirts of Henderson in an abandoned subdivision, almost all of the homes unfinished. Apparently, the builder went bankrupt, and everything was left as it was. According to the property records, none of the homes should be inhabitable, yet there was one clearly with lights blazing. Brick was obviously a cocky prick, not believing anyone would investigate or give a shit about him occupying the home.

"We leave the bikes here," said Ghost to the other men as they stood at the bottom of the surrounding foothills. "Walk in, use the homes as your cover. Zulu? You and Gunner take out the guys on the outside quietly if you can." He raised the binoculars with NVG and cursed under his breath.

"What's wrong?" asked Eagle.

"I see two men on the roof of the house behind them." Eagle nodded, lifting his rifle, the big scope with the silencer making it nearly impossible to hear. Both men would be dead before they even heard the faint sounds. Gathering the first man in his sights, he looked at his brother standing next to him, both rifles settled on the hood of the SUV.

"I got the right," said Hawk.

"Got the left, three, two, one..." *Thwap. Thwap.* He fist-bumped his brother, grinning. "Nice job."

"Damn," said Knuckles, "that's some fine shooting."

"Thank you, sir," said Hawk.

"Alright, let's go." Knuckles and his men allowed Ghost and his team to take the lead, following them as they used the homes for easy cover. With the darkness of the desert sky and none of the other homes lit up, it was an easy approach.

Hawk watched as Gunner and Zulu took out four men swiftly, never raising their weapons. As they let each body fall to the ground, another man approached from the side of the house, his weapon pointed at Zulu's back. Unfortunately for him, he never saw Whiskey coming. With two quick swipes of his wrist, the large bowie knife cut through the artery at his neck and then at the one in his groin.

"Thanks, brother," said Zulu.

"You're getting slow, old man," grinned Whiskey.

Opening the front door slowly, Eagle and Hawk took the lead, walking quietly through the foyer to enter the kitchen where the other two men were drinking and eating. Neither was able to make a sound before they were dropped by the silent weapons of the twins.

Hearing the blaring sound of a football game coming from another room, Ghost directed them silently down the hallway. As they got closer, they could hear a man yelling and directing at least one woman.

"Fucking on your knees, bitch!" he yelled. "Suck it. Suck my cock. Get it hard, you cunt! You... do what I told you... shove that up her ass."

"B-Brick, please don't make me. It will hurt her," cried the small voice.

"I said…" *Crunch!* The sound of his own bones breaking confused the man for a moment, then clearing his vision and wiping the blood from his face, he pushed the woman from his lap, her body lax, almost lifeless.

"Who the fuck do you think you are? Cobra?" he yelled toward the kitchen. Hearing nothing, he swallowed hard but showed no signs of panic. A serious underestimation on his part.

"Your friends have been neutralized," said Hawk. "Now you're next."

"You will fucking die, you stupid fuck. I have friends you can't even…"

"Oh, you mean like Dawg and Gutierrez?" said Eagle. The man's face paled, and he looked around the room, suddenly filled with huge men.

"You got this?" asked Ghost. Eagle and Hawk nodded. "Let's go, ladies. We're getting you out of here."

"Nobody touches my bitches," he grinned. The sounds of gunfire brought a small smile to his lips until he realized there were more men than were in this room.

"We'll get the other girls out of here," said Gunner. "Have fun with this prick."

"Where is Dawg?" asked Ghost.

"Fuck you."

"You're not my type, and even if you were, that dick ain't big enough to even make me smile."

"Fuck you."

"Limited vocabulary is a sure sign of a lack of intelligence, or his mother intentionally dropped him on his head as an infant," said Hawk. "I'm going to guess it was both."

"What the hell do you want? How do I know you?"

"You don't know me," said Eagle. "But I'm marrying someone you know. Someone you hurt intentionally."

"And I'm marrying one of your offspring," said Hawk.

"One of my... What the fuck? Look, if I got fucking kids, I don't know about it. You know how bitches are... always claimin' they missed a pill or some shit. I ain't got no kids I claim."

"Tinley and Keegan," said Eagle. That brought an eyebrow raise from him. His face started to smile, and then he frowned, looking at the twins.

"You fucking tellin' me one of you is marrying that old bitch, and the other is fucking with her daughter?" He laughed, his head falling back to the headboard. "And you call me fucked up? That's sick, man."

"You like to hit women, don't you?" said Hawk. He grinned and shrugged his shoulders. Hawk brought up his weapon, firing into his right knee. He screamed in agony, gripping the shattered knee. "Answer me. You like to hit women?"

"What the fuck. So what! They don't do what they're fuckin' told, they get hit, taught a lesson." *Thwap!* Eagle hit the other knee. Another scream of agony as he rolled to his side.

"You still have a chance. Where is Dawg?" asked Eagle.

"Fuck you!" he screamed. "You think I'm going to tell you anything?! He'll fucking kill you. He'll fucking kill you all!"

"You aren't that important, dude. He just wants money, drugs, and women, and we're about to take away all of that."

"You're doin' all this for two fucking sluts!" Hawk started to step forward and then took a breath, waiting for his moment. "Bet that little bitch is hot now, ain't she? She was gonna be a sweet addition to my enterprise. Get her fuckin' the brothers at thirteen or fourteen. She good in bed? She suck your dick good?" *Thwap! Thwap!*

Two shots fired, one into each shoulder as Hawk just stared at the man. His body writhing in pain, agony etched on his features.

"Where is Dawg?" asked Eagle again.

"I don't know. He lives in the mountains. Only comes down to get a few girls now and then, money, some blow. That's it." Eagle walked slowly toward the man who dared touch his woman. Who'd made her lose two babies. The man who made her fearful of every man after him.

"You're going to die now, but just know that Tinley will be my wife. She will carry my babies, and we will live a long, happy life together. My brother will marry Keegan, who is nothing like you, nothing. They will be blessed with so many babies, it will make your head spin. Except you'll be dead." He raised his gun and fired three times directly into his head.

From behind him, he heard another three shots fired into the man's body, turning to see his brother with a grave expression.

"We both deserved the kill," said Hawk. Eagle nodded as they walked out. The front lawn was covered in half-naked, starved, drug-addled women.

"Get the girls to the lawn across the street," said Ghost. "We're gonna blow the house with the drugs and money. Call the cops and the feds. Tell them you worked off a tip and got here in time to save the women, but apparently, a rival gang killed the guys and blew the house."

"You should take the credit, brother," said Knuckles. Ghost shook his head.

"Nope, don't need it; don't want it. Get the girls to safety. Get them to their families. That's all the credit I need."

"You boys leavin' tomorrow?" asked Knuckles. Ghost nodded. "Well, it's been a fucking pleasure, brother. Leave the bikes at the hotel. We'll pick them up from there. Just take a taxi to the airport. We'll let you know if we hear anything from Dawg or Gutierrez. Watch your backs, brother. Dawg won't take this lyin' down."

"I've still got a few connections with the feds. I'll see if they can make sure Gutierrez only sees this as an accident in the desert. Maybe paint it that Brick turned on his men or something."

"He'd believe it. Fucking bastard was crazy." Knuckles looked around at the girls, now being carefully loaded in the vehicles, their tiny bodies clearly abused and filled with drugs.

"Let us know how the girls are, man. We really want to know." He clasped the other man's hand and gripped it firmly. "Take care, brother."

The Aces watched as Ghost and his men took off into the night. When the women were loaded into the vehicles and on their way to the hospital, Knuckles stepped back from the house, knowing it was going to blow. He smiled as debris and flames filled the sky. Those bastards must have put fifty pounds of explosives in there. He could only shake his head and grin. One of his younger members walked up, grinning.

"Who were those guys?" he asked.

"Those were real, live superheroes, son. Bona fide fucking superheroes."

CHAPTER TWENTY-FIVE

Tinley woke to the feel of warm flesh melting against her back, big muscled arms enveloping her body, the rough meaty palm of one hand splayed out against her stomach, pulling her flush against something thick and hard. She moaned, expecting to wake from the dream, instead feeling the familiar warm lips against the back of her neck.

"You really should be careful. I'm engaged to a hot younger man with a fiery temper," she smiled. Ty said nothing, simply lifting her leg back, up and over his hip, sliding inside her heat. The heel of his hand pressed against her, massaging her clit as he pounded in silence inside her.

"Oh, oh, yes, Ty..." she moaned, feeling the intensity in her belly build, the feeling of him filling her as he drilled into her mercilessly. She heard him growl and felt the release inside her, her own orgasm flowing in time with his. Flipping her around to face him, he buried his hands in her hair, taking her mouth violently, tasting her, then gently nipping, nibbling, pulling back to look into her eyes.

Tinley looked at him with concern. He'd said nothing, just attacked her in the most loving, needful way, but still, he attacked. His eyes were filled with unshed tears. Kissing his nose, then both eyes, then his lips once more, she gripped his face.

"Are you okay, baby?" she asked quietly.

"I killed him, honey. I had to. Don't hate me, please. I couldn't stand it if you hated me," he said.

"Hate you? Ty, nothing you could ever do would make me hate you. Ghost said you would be eliminating him. I knew what that meant. I understand, and believe me, I was okay with it. I'm sorry you had to do it, but I'm damn sure glad it's done."

"Baby, baby," he cried against her breast. "I love you so much, Tinley. He was a piece of shit. More than thirty girls, all underage in that house, half-naked, hooked on the drugs he was selling. We got them out, but they'll never be the same, none of them."

"But you got them out, Ty. That's what you have to remember. You're giving them a chance to find a new normal. It's far more than they had yesterday." She held his head to her naked chest, feeling the wetness of his tears. It nearly shattered her to see this big, strong, fearless man crying over ridding the earth of someone like Brick.

"I missed you," she whispered. "I missed you so much it hurt. I've never felt that kind of emptiness, even when I sent Keegan to summer camp. I know it was only for a few nights, but I couldn't sleep. I would reach out for you and weep because you weren't here."

"I'm so sorry, baby girl," he said, pulling her to his chest.

"I will never, ever question this love, Ty. Never. I am in love with you, and you are in love with me. Done. I want to marry you and have as many babies as my body will let me have," she grinned.

"Really?" he smiled, looking down at her.

"Really. I had several long talks with Grace and Bree and the other girls as well, but I figured out really quick that I wouldn't be able to live, be able to breathe without you." He was quiet for a moment, and then she spoke again. "You know what I want?"

"What, baby? Tell me. Anything you want, I'll give you," he said, kissing the top of her head.

"I want to get married February 2nd, right out back, overlooking the valley. I just want our friends and family, a quick simple ceremony. I want Amanda to sing, I want George to walk me down the aisle, and I want to see your face standing at the end of my walk, looking at me like you do, loving me. I want to have a simple quiet dinner, and then I want to go to that cabin Ghost said we could have and lock the doors for a week. When we emerge, we're going to have a baby or two started," she smiled.

Eagle couldn't help but laugh a nervous laugh

"Oh, sweetie," he said, kissing her. "I will give you anything you want, and since February 2nd is only a few weeks away, it's perfect. Maybe Hawk and Keegan will want to get married at the same time?"

"I can't think of anything better," she smiled. She wiggled beneath his big body, turning him to lie on top of her, her legs spread wide, wrapping around his hips. "Now, I think you have at least one more in you before we sleep." Ty slid his dick inside her once again, moaning at the feeling of that slick heat surrounding him.

"Baby, I got more than one more in me. Buckle up, buttercup. It's gonna be a late night."

CHAPTER TWENTY-SIX

Keegan heard the sound of the door and gasped, gripping the covers under her chin. She grabbed her cell phone, ready to hit the SOS key for the guys in the barn. She tried to calm her beating heart, but she had no idea who might be coming into the cottage so late.

"Baby," she heard the soft call. Throwing back the covers, she leapt from the bed and raced out into the living room, throwing herself in Ryan's arms, wrapping her legs around his waist. She plastered kisses across his face, finally landing on his lips and melting into him.

"I missed you so much," she cried against his lips. Tears trailed down her cheeks, Ryan kissing them away as quickly as they fell.

"Oh, sweet baby, don't cry. I missed you too, honey," he said, settling on the sofa with her still wrapped around him. "Baby, I-I had to..."

"I know. I know you killed him, and I know you had to. I don't care, Ryan. All I cared about was you coming back to me."

"My love, I will always come back to you, always. I love you so much, Keegan." Ryan couldn't believe how much he'd missed Keegan. She was right. Vegas was filled with hot women willing to get drunk and do anything. Brides looking for their last big fling. He didn't give a shit about any of them. All he kept looking for was Keegan, and she wasn't in Las Vegas.

"Is everyone else okay? Ty? Ghost? All the others?"

"They're all good, baby. Everyone is fine, no issues. We only have to worry about Dawg now, but we'll find him. In the meantime, you're going to stay right here with me." She nodded, wiping the tears from her face as she kissed him once again.

"Valerie showed up at the clinic," she said quietly.

"Damn," he groaned, leaning his head back against the sofa. "Did she cause trouble?"

"Not really, Gabi saw her for a cold or something, and when she demanded to see you, she told her you were out of town with your fiancée." That brought a much-needed laugh to his lips.

"Good for Gabi," he smiled.

"Yea, she told her that she wasn't welcome at the clinic any longer. Told her to find a new doctor. I worry about what lengths she might go to, though."

"Don't worry about her, baby. I'm going to have a conversation with her and get this settled. I'm not sure what bag of crazy she ate from, but this is ridiculous. She was always the one that said she preferred women to men. Men were just a distraction for her. She knew where I stood."

"I know, baby," she said, kissing his neck, trailing down to his chest. Keegan lifted his t-shirt over his head, her hand sliding down to his belt buckle, unzipping his jeans, and pulling him out. "I need you."

"Fuck, Keegan," Keegan slid down his body, tugging at his jeans as he lifted his hips. Removing his boots, she pulled them all the way off and spread his knees wide, placing herself in between them. Her fingers walked up his thighs, reaching out to stroke his velvety, hot skin.

Placing soft kisses on his heavy balls, she licked up the center, following all the way to the tip of

his big purple head.

Ryan looked down at his beautiful girl, her mouth wrapped around his cock, that tongue

working magic on him. He wrapped her hair around one fist and tugged, reaching down to

squeeze her nipple. Keegan was sucking him so hard, her cheeks were hollowed.

"Kee, fuck, baby, I'm gonna..." She nodded, giving her okay for him to release. The

warm salty flavor of Ryan filled her mouth. She swallowed every last drop as he shuddered

against her lips. Looking up, she grinned, licking her lips. Ryan lifted her from the floor,

slamming her against the sofa and burying his still hard cock inside her.

"I fucking missed you so much," he said against her lips. "There were women

everywhere, but not one of them was you, not even fucking close. You're mine, Keegan, mine

and mine alone. I will never touch another woman, never."

"Good," she said breathlessly as she wiggled her hips against him, "because no man will

ever compare to you, Ryan. I love you, and I want to marry you."

"When?" he asked excitedly.

"February 2nd. Mom is going to marry Ty that day. Can we do it then? Together?"

"Fuck yea, baby," he growled. Lifting her from the sofa still wrapped around his cock, he

carried her to the bedroom, laying her between the sheets. It was only moments before

Keegan shattered around his dick, her sweet pussy constricting him, making him blow again.

"God, woman, you are so amazing. I love you, Keegan. I never thought I could love anyone like this," he said, trailing kisses over each breast.

"I know," she said with a sniff. "I get emotional every time I think about it. I missed you so bad. I would come back here to the cottage just so I could grab one of your shirts and smell it. I finally just wore the black Harley shirt under your Marine Corps sweatshirt. It felt like you were hugging me."

"Awe, baby," he laughed, "that's so sweet. Honey, you can wear my clothes any time you want. I'm sure they look better on you than me. But when we're alone, love, I want you naked, always."

"Always," she whispered, "I like the sound of that."

"Always," he said, kissing her forehead. "Always." Kisses to her temples. "Always." Kisses to her nose. "Always." Kisses to her lips.

"Forever."

CHAPTER TWENTY-SEVEN

His face turned a horrid shade of purple, one thick vein pulsing at the top of his forehead. Bloodshot eyes stared at the man across from him, fury building by the second. Thick fingers covered in big silver rings slammed into his side once more.

"P-please, please, Dawg. I don't know what happened. I wasn't there. All I know is Brick and the others are dead. The girls were taken, the money and drugs blown," he groaned.

"Well, you shoulda been fucking there!" He lifted the pistol and emptied it into the man writhing on the floor. A few moments later, another man walked in, staring down at the dead body of his friend.

"What... the... fuck... happened?" he asked.

"I don't know," Dawg started to come toward him, his big fists raised once more. "W-wait, wait, I have something for you, though." He dropped his fists, waiting. Pulling out his phone, the man held up a picture of several people appearing to enjoy a party.

"What the fuck is that?" he asked.

"Don't you recognize her? That's her. That's the bitch that Brick used to fuck. The one that did our books. I don't recognize the others, but her I do. Look at the eyes. She always had these amazing eyes." Dawg grabbed the phone from his hand, staring at the picture. Yea, that was her. The bitch who gave him away. She'd been gone ten years. Why did she have to tell the club about his secret stash? The only reason she wasn't killed back then was that she was so good with numbers. Brick would have long since thrown her to the brothers, but Dawg convinced him to keep her healthy.

She had a kid, a girl. Maybe the other woman in the picture was the daughter. The twin guys looked like a couple of preppy doughboys.

"Where was this taken?" he asked.

"Someplace called Club Steel in a little town in Virginia. It's just some bar and restaurant. It was taken New Year's Eve, so chances are good they live in the area." Dawg nodded, still staring at the picture. This fucking bitch was the reason he was in hiding, and if she had anything to do with the killing of Brick, he would make her suffer pain beyond her imagination.

"How many guys we still got?" he asked.

"Just three," said the other man. "Nine were killed at the house, including Brick. After that, five of them left. No clue where they went. It's just me, Cash, and Toad."

"Fuck," he muttered. "The girls?"

"Gone. Whoever blew the house took the girls and got them to hospitals. Some of them might be able to ID us, Dawg. We've all been in and out of that house, used some of those girls. They could..."

"I know what they can do," he growled. "We can't kill thirty girls. We don't have the manpower."

"What do you want to do about her?" he said, pointing to the phone.

"We're gonna take a drive east. Tell the boys to pack their bags. We're leaving Nevada. We're gonna find the bitch who posted that photo, and then we're gonna take care of her. When we're done, we'll head to Mexico. Gutierrez promised me a place to lay low."

The other man nodded but knew this was going to be a fool's errand. If they were offered sanctuary in Mexico, they needed to take that offer now, not later. But there would be no convincing Dawg of that. He didn't know who this girl, Valerie, was or how she was connected to Tinley, but she had no clue what was headed her way.

CHAPTER TWENTY-EIGHT

Hawk walked into the kitchen, seeing his brother and Skull seated at the table. None of the others were up yet, but he knew they would be coming down soon.

"You two willing to take a ride with me?" he asked. Skull looked up, somewhat concerned.

"Sure, always got your back, brother. Where are we going?" he asked.

"I need to have a conversation with that bitch, Valerie. She came to the clinic while we were gone asking for me and basically threatened Keegan. I won't put up with it. I want a couple of witnesses so I can make myself perfectly clear to her and protect myself legally."

"I'll definitely sit back and watch that," said his brother. "Let's go. George? If Tinley comes down, will you let her know we're running an errand. Be back in an hour." George nodded as they walked out the door.

"You got an address?" asked Skull. Hawk nodded.

"Ace looked it up for me. She lives in a little house in the valley with three other girls. It's why I want my own witnesses."

The three men took the SUV down the mountain toward the address indicated on the paper. The houses were small and not very well maintained, obviously lower income. Pulling in front, Hawk stepped out with his brother and Skull, making their way to the front door. It wasn't even eight a.m. yet, so he figured she would be home, either drunk or hung over. He knocked, and when no one answered, knocked again. Hearing the chain removed, he stepped back.

"Well, well, well," said Valerie. "Brought your stud brother and a spare. I'm hardly awake, but let me get a cup of coffee in me, and I'll service you good, baby. I knew you'd crawl back."

"I'm not here for you, Valerie. I don't want anything to do with you. I told you that." Her face flashed with anger, and she curled a lip, glaring at him and the other two men. "I'm gonna make this perfectly fucking clear. Stay away from the clinic, stay away from Club Steel, and listen carefully."

Hawk took a step forward, his big body hovering over hers as two other women looked on from the living room. He intentionally made his size more intimidating by having Eagle and Skull behind him.

"I will never touch you again. If you ever threaten Keegan or any member of my family again, I will make sure that you regret it. You are nothing to me, Valerie. You never were. You were a willing piece of ass who got something from me, just like I got something from you. That's it. It was nothing special, nothing I want more of."

"You're a fucking piece of shit and a sorry fuck," she said, trying to smile. "You think you're hot shit because you have an identical twin, and you're surrounded by all those do-gooders? You're nothing, nothing!"

"Fine. I'm nothing. Then leave me alone, and do not ever come near me or Keegan again. I mean it, Valerie." He stepped closer and leaned down close to her ear. She jerked a bit in fear and then settled. "I can make you disappear, and no one will ever find you. Don't fuck

with me or my family."

"Whatever, *Hawk*," she huffed. One of the girls behind her walked toward the door.

"Val, let it go. You don't even really want him; you're just pissed that Keegan got him.

Let this go, or you're going to end up with more trouble than you can handle." Val whipped

around, glaring at her friend.

"You're supposed to be on my side!" she yelled.

"I am on your side. Look, you're a bi-sexual woman who doesn't give a shit about him. I

love you, Val, but you want to own everyone until you don't. You're just pissed that he cut you

loose, before you cut him loose. Let it go." The woman stared at her and then turned back to

the door.

"You know what, I don't even give a shit anymore. Your cock wasn't all that great

anyway. There are plenty of other places for my friends and I to party. Live your life, lover boy.

I'll be sitting here grinning when you toss her aside, or she tosses you aside."

"Gonna be a long wait, Val. Keegan and I are getting married. I never meant to hurt

you, Val. I'm sorry if I did. Really, I am."

"Like I said, Hawk, whatever. Is that all? Can I go back to my coffee now?" she said,

smirking.

"Yea, that's all." The door slammed in his face, and he stepped back, letting out a long

slow breath. He felt his brother's hand gripping one shoulder and Skull gripping the other.

"I'm proud of you, Ryan," said Ty.

"Me too, man," said Skull. "That was what we would refer to as a transformational moment. Ten years of growth in ten minutes, brother. Amazing." Hawk grinned at his friend and nodded.

"I mean it, you know. Keegan is it for me. We're getting married, right next to Ty and Tinley."

"Man, the whole club has turned into one big love fest," said Skull, starting the truck once again. "You guys are finding your better halves faster than a jack rabbit. The number of rug rats running around our place is gonna be overwhelming." Ty chuckled, nodding at the other man.

"Yea, I hope so. I want kids right away, and so does Tinley finally! She knows she'll only have a few years where she'll be able to have kids, but with any luck, we'll have twins, and that would be enough for me."

"Damn! You're hoping for twins?" asked Skull.

"Oh, yea. Definitely hoping for twins," said Hawk and Eagle together, laughing as they did.

"You guys are twisted."

"Nope. Man, having a twin means you always had someone to play with, you always had a fight buddy, you always had someone to cover for you..."

"Switch places with you," laughed Ty. "It's awesome, and I hope I have kids who get to experience that. I love watching Wade and Tyler grow. They're just crawling and sitting up, but you can see them already helping each other as they do. Plus, all these kids are going to be close in age, which will make for instant playmates."

"I guess I never thought about it," said Skull. "I mean, I'm thirty-seven and probably should think about it. I'm just a little shyer than you guys, don't jump into the pool as quickly. I'm also not the pretty boy of the group. We all got scars, but mine are visible." Ty chuckled.

"Brother, no one was shyer than Ace, and look what happened with him and Charlie. You just gotta put yourself out there, Skull. I watch you, brother; you spend twelve hours a day in the shop. I mean, you do amazing work, but you gotta make time for you too. Any woman who is worth your time won't give two shits about that scar on your face. You're a solid dude, man." He nodded, wiping a big hand over his face.

Fifteen years in the Coast Guard had made him tough and lonely. As the biggest guy on the boat, he usually had the duty to board a ship first, and that earned him the nice long scar from his ear around his jaw, stopping just below his bottom lip. It looked like a big fishhook.

Starting a relationship was tough when he was in the guard. He was always at sea, which made for very challenging attempts at long-term relationships. He wasn't the guy to fuck everything in sight. He needed a real connection with a woman to take her to bed. Besides the fact that he was gone all the time, he was a big man. Hell, all of the guys were. But where Zulu was tall and muscled, and Gunner was tall and built, Skull was tall, wide, muscled, and thick. Skull was six-foot-five and two hundred and fifty pounds.

His chest was the classic example of a barrel-chested man, his shoulders so wide he had to turn sideways to walk through doors. He looked more like a professional wrestler than a coastie.

Giving more thought to what the twins said, he reminded himself that it was a week past New Years, but maybe he would make a resolution a few days too late. Maybe this year, he would vow to find love. Step outside his comfort zone and actively seek someone. Maybe, or maybe not.

CHAPTER TWENTY-NINE

By the time they returned from the valley and visiting with Valerie and her roommates, everyone was happily eating breakfast, welcoming everyone home. Tinley and Keegan jumped up to kiss the boys hello.

"Where did you run off to so early?" asked Keegan.

"Eagle, Skull, and I made a little visit to Valerie," he said. He waited for her to be angry with him, but she only smiled.

"How did that go?" He shrugged his shoulders.

"I think I got my point across, but I don't know. She was a real bitch about it. Thankfully, even one of her roommates came forward and told her to back down. I think if it doesn't get better, we might want Kat to file a restraining order."

"Already done," said Kat.

"What?" Hawk looked up at her, surprised.

"Gabi asked me to do it because of her behavior at the clinic. She should get served today, stating she is not to step foot on any property belonging to the Steel Patriots. She is not allowed to be within one hundred yards of Gabi, Doc, you, or Keegan. If she violates the order, she will be arrested and prosecuted. Thanks to Ace, we have recordings of her threats in the clinic."

"Holy shit, I think I love you," he grinned.

"She's my wife, asshole," growled Whiskey, kissing his wife's forehead. He winked at Keegan and punched Hawk playfully in the arm.

"Thank you, Kat, seriously. I think this woman is unhinged, and I just don't know what she's capable of." Kat nodded, patting his hand, and smiling. Having a lawyer in their midst was becoming increasingly advantageous. They didn't want to have to use her services often, but it was damn sure nice to have her there when they needed her.

"Hey, Skull," said Tango. "We got a call from a woman who wants to buy a bike for her brother as a gift. It's a really cool story. He served twenty-five years in the Army, supporting her and their little brother, who is now in the Army as well. Basically, the guy sacrificed everything to make sure his siblings stayed together and yet still served his country."

"That's the kind of thing I love working on. Does she know how expensive this is gonna be?" He nodded at the other man.

"Yea, man, she invented some sort of software program that sold for millions. She doesn't really have to work anymore but does some contract stuff on the side. She lives in Seattle now but will be moving out this way in the spring to be closer to her brothers. She sent some basic information and a deposit. I told her we'd let you draw up some ideas and e-mail them to her."

"Fucking awesome, man. What's her name in case I get an e-mail and don't know who it is?"

"Willa, uh, let me see," he said, scrolling through his phone, "Willa Ross."

"Okay, Willa," he repeated.

He liked the sound of her name on his lips, and it made him smile. If she were the younger sister of a man who served twenty-five years, she could be anywhere from twenty-five years old to forty-two years old. He wasn't sure why he was even thinking about her age, but for some reason, her name tickled his tongue, and he looked forward to meeting Willa Ross.

Ghost walked into the kitchen with Ace on his heels.

"Listen up," he said, looking at the group. "The mess in Vegas was taken care of thanks to the Aces and the local police. Feds aren't thrilled we screwed with Gutierrez, but they're not saying anything either. Problem is, someone spotted Dawg and three other men riding out of Vegas. They were positive it was him. Ace followed a probable pattern of traffic and thinks he got him on camera in Kansas City a night ago, checking into a motel."

"He's coming this way," whispered Tinley as she snuggled into Ty's big body. Ghost nodded.

"I wish I could lie to you, honey, but I won't do that. It looks like he is. But hear me loud and clear, we're gonna be ready for him."

CHAPTER THIRTY

Parking their motorcycles behind the small cabin they'd rented, Dawg and the three men went inside to find a clean, well-furnished space. Toad started a fire in the massive stone fireplace and dropped the groceries they'd purchased in the last town.

"Don't make yourselves too fucking comfortable," grumbled Dawg. "We're gonna find this bitch Valerie and then get Tinley. I'm gonna kill that whore."

The others just nodded, tired and cold from the long drive on the bikes. All they really wanted to do was sleep and shower. For Coop, he'd been part of the Bastards his entire fifty-two years. He was road weary, his body feeling much older than it actually was. He'd contemplated on more than one occasion leaving Dawg, but the truth was this was all he'd ever known.

It wasn't much different for Cash and Toad. Both men were nearly sixty now. Neither had ever been married, although they'd had their fair share of club pussy, drugs, and alcohol, and it showed on their weary, weathered faces. When Dawg got into selling the drugs and pussy, they'd looked the other way. When the girls started getting younger and younger, they'd been reluctant but, under the influence of the drugs, didn't turn it away.

Now, they all felt they were in so deep, there was no turning back. Despite the betrayal of Dawg stealing from the coffers of the club, they'd followed him into the hills, hiding out until they could form the club once more. The longer they were in hiding, the more apparent it became that there would never be another Bastards club.

"Where does the bitch Valerie live?" asked Dawg.

"Not far, but she works closer. A bar around the corner. We can walk, maybe convince her to have some fun with us and then figure out what she knows," said Coop. Dawg grinned, a lewd despicable grin, and even Coop stepped back. This man enjoyed giving pain and especially giving pain to women.

"I'd suggest we shower if we want her to come back with us," said Toad.

"Fine, make your asses smell pretty. I'm gonna get a shower and some sleep. Have her back here by dark. All the better if she brings her friends," said Dawg. "Cash? Show her your pecker if you have to."

Cash grinned at his old friend. Of the four of them, he was probably still the best-looking. Although he was definitely gray, he had a hard body, and more than that, he packed a ten-inch dick that the ladies loved to ride. He wasn't a man who needed pharmaceutical help to get it up, just a little rub and a hot mouth.

Coop felt his stomach dip and wanted desperately to run like hell. Instead, he took the first bathroom, showering off the dirt and sweat of the road. Leaving their kuttes at the cabin, the three men sported clean jeans and shirts, their long hair combed back and their beards somewhat trimmed.

It was cold outside, but nothing they couldn't manage with just a sweatshirt with a hood. The walk to the small bar only took about five minutes. The space was dark and cramped. A few locals hunched over the bar, looking as though it were the end of days.

Glancing down at his phone, Coop nodded toward the girl behind the bar, and the others followed.

"Well, hello, handsomes," she grinned at the men, "what can I get 'ya?"

Cash smiled at the girl, taking in her body, soaking up every inch she was offering to them. She wasn't very big, but she had a full rack, definitely enhanced. Her bleach blonde hair was long, her lips full with bright red lipstick on them.

"I'd like a side of you, sugar," said Cash.

"Oh, honey," she grinned, "not sure you could handle me. I like my men young, virile, thick, and lasting all night long." Cash stood and unzipped his jeans, pulling out the long snake that was his cock. Valerie's eyes grew wide, a smile spread across her face, and she laughed.

"Well, alright then, you got what I can definitely use," she laughed. "What about your friends? They gonna join us or just watch?"

"No, baby, you get all three of us for the price of one," he smiled.

"Sounds good. I get off in twenty minutes, but, in the meantime," she said, grinning at Cash, "why don't you meet me in the lady's room for a quickie so I don't cream my jeans while we wait." Cash barked out a loud laugh and nodded, winking at Toad and Coop. He followed the little slut to the lady's room, her ass wiggling as she walked. Once inside, she pushed down her jeans, laying them on the sink, and spread her legs wide for him.

"Fuck girl, you want this old dick bad, don't you?" he growled as he unzipped, pulling out his already stiff cock.

"Yea, I do. You got a problem with that?" she huffed.

"Nope."

He pulled out a condom, wrapping it up as always, and slammed into her, feeling her not-so-tight pussy take all of him. This bitch was experienced, and she enjoyed a little pain with her pleasure. Gripping her hair, he forced her head back and sucked on her neck, moving down. With his other hand, he pushed up the sweater and shoved the bra over one full tit. Biting down hard, she yelped with pain, and he only grinned.

"Keep quiet, honey. You wanted my big dick. Take it," he said, slamming her into the mirror, his big cock definitely hurting her. She nodded, not able to say anything as he pounded into her, abusing her body in a way she enjoyed. "Don't you fucking cum until I say so." He growled, gripping her throat. She could only nod, his hands making her body immobile. Cash bent down, violently taking her mouth as he bit into her lip, drawing blood. He heard her mewling and grinned.

"I need to..." she pleaded.

"Do it," he yelled. A deep rumbling roar released from him as he shot into the condom. She gasped as her own orgasm rocked her little body, but he didn't even allow the aftershocks to settle. He quickly pulled out, tossing the condom in the wastebasket. Zipping up, he looked at her body, the disheveled clothing, marks on her neck and chest, and grinned.

"You're a great fuck, honey. Can't wait for me and the boys to have another go with you."

"So are you," she smiled. "What's your name?"

"Cash like the bills." She giggled, and he grinned back at her. She had no clue what was coming for her.

"Valerie. I'll see you boys outside in twenty, fifteen minutes." He nodded, opening the door to see another woman looking pissed.

"What the fuck are you doing, Val?" asked the girl.

"Chill. He's got a dick like an anaconda. The old man definitely knows how to work it," she smiled, fixing her hair in the mirror. "I'm gonna have a little party with him and his friends. I need this release after today."

"Val, you're playing with fire. Those are grown men, not boys. They're covered head to toe with tattoos and not the good kind. Honey, don't do this," begged the other woman.

"Jesus! What are you, my mother? Back the fuck off! I deserve this."

She walked out of the lady's room and stepped behind the bar. The three men smiling at her, her new fuckbuddy looking her up and down. She never thought she'd sleep with somebody his age, but he was pretty damn good, and if he could get it up again in another twenty minutes, they were gonna be great friends.

Finishing her shift, she waved at her friend, who frowned, watching Val leave with the three men.

"Where you boys staying?" she asked.

"Cabin up ahead," growled one of them.

"What's your name?" she asked.

"None of your fucking business." She looked at Cash, who smiled and shrugged his shoulders.

"No problem, don't need to know your names to suck your dick. Three of you, one of me, this should be fun." Cash opened the door, Dawg seated in the big leather chair by the fire as if he were ruling a small country. She stepped in and smiled nervously.

"Four?" she asked, raising an eyebrow. "Okay, I'm willing." Dawg stood, moving toward her as Cash closed the door, locking it behind him.

"Willing or not, bitch, you're going to give me what I want."

CHAPTER THIRTY-ONE

Tinley sat across from Ghost, explaining all the things she'd found in the books. She transferred all the discrepancies and potential cost savings to a separate spreadsheet and then showed him what the changes in the vendors would do for them.

"I can't believe this," he said, looking at the numbers. "The beer vendor has cost us more than twenty thousand dollars in the last five years, and the liquor vendor is worse. Our food vendors are more than those two combined." Tinley nodded.

"I know it's hard to hear, but it's true." Ghost dialed the speaker phone, waiting for the familiar voice of the salesperson to come on.

"Ghost! It's so good to hear from you!" came the bellowing voice.

"Ben, got a problem here," he snarled.

"O-oh, I hate to hear that. Did we not send enough bottles?" Ghost looked at Tinley and nodded.

"Ben? This is Tinley. I'm the CPA for the Steel Patriots and all their businesses."

"O-okay, I thought you handled the books, Ghost."

"Apparently not," he grinned up at Tinley.

"Ben, I've been reviewing all the books, and it seems not only have you cheated us on some of the shipments, but you've been over-delivering on other shipments."

"Wh-what, Ghost, you know this isn't right. We've been doing business together for the last six years. I don't know who this woman is, but it's obvious she doesn't know what she's talking about."

"This woman is a highly intelligent, highly capable professional. At Ghost's request, I reviewed the invoices for the last five years. You haven't been honest with him, Ben. Now, in the interest of protecting my client, I'm going to have to recommend that we terminate our business relationship."

"Ghost? Tell me you're not gonna listen to this bitch!"

"Brother, if you want to keep those capped teeth of yours, I'd be damn careful what you say next. Tinley is marrying one of my men, and she's part of this family. By your actions, you're telling me everything I need to know. We're cone." He hung up the phone and dialed the next number.

"Roy here," came the gravelly, smoky voice.

"Roy, it's Ghost."

"Hey, man, what's up? Having another party? Need another shipment?" he asked. Ghost only rolled his eyes, looking at Tinley again.

"Roy, my name is Tinley, and I am the new CPA for the Steel Patriots. I've been doing a review of their books for the last five years, and I have some questions about your invoicing." There was dead silence on the other end of the line, and then they heard the sounds of papers being shuffled.

"So, uh, is this about the napkins and things? I can explain that, Ghost. Listen, I promised it would be comped, but then my boss said I couldn't do that, so..."

"So, you lied and charged me anyway?" he roared into the phone. Nothing pissed him off more than someone taking advantage of him and his family. "You don't get it, do you, asshole? This is a family business. We share the profits, and the majority go into our fund to help others. You've basically knowingly stolen from me, my family, and other families in need."

"Hey, I'll talk to my boss."

"I'm sorry," said Tinley. "We're going to be terminating our services with you. If you send another automatic, unauthorized shipment, we will legally have the right to retain that shipment... without cost. My suggestion is you cease those automatic deliveries immediately."

"Right, sure. I am sorry about this," he murmured.

"No," said Ghost. "You're sorry you got caught. You're not sorry you did it. That's the difference." The line clicked off, and Tinley smiled at Ghost.

"Nice job. Go ahead and set us up with the vendors you know and keep a close watch on them." She nodded as someone knocked on the door. Entering the room were Razor, Tango, and Skull. "Boys, have a seat. Tinley has some questions about some of our vendors for the shop and the invoices."

"Sure, no problem. What's up?" asked Skull.

"Well, I know nothing of the garage or motorcycle business, so a lot of this is probably going to sound stupid."

"Nothing stupid about asking questions, honey. If you can save us money, we're all for it. Just remember that these are custom bikes and cars, so we don't skimp on the parts. Everything is top of the line, top quality shit."

"Understood, I promise," she said. "So, do you guys review the invoices when you get the parts?" All three squirmed a bit in their seats, grinning at her.

"Well, to be honest with you, no. We pretty much know what we paid, and everything gets tacked into the cost of the bikes. Our profit is huge, so I don't think that's an issue." Smiling, she politely nodded.

"Okay, what should a carburetor cost for the average bike build?"

"Maybe a hundred bucks," said Tango, looking at the others, who all nodded.

"Okay, and forks for the average bike?"

"Anywhere from seven hundred to fifteen hundred, depending on the bike style, size, that sort of thing," said Skull.

"And a tank for a custom bike, minus the paint job."

"Again, depending on the bike, fifty to two hundred bucks," said Skull.

"Okay, let me tell you what the invoices say. For the last fifty-three carburetors you purchased, you paid an average of two hundred and thirty-seven dollars."

"What!" all three men yelled. She grinned, nodding again.

"For the forks, it was an average cost of two thousand, eight hundred and eleven dollars."

"Fuck," moaned Razor.

"And the tanks... the tanks were a whopping nine hundred dollars and eight cents," she grinned. "You guys are getting raped on the costs of the parts, and I'm only looking at three that seemed high to me. I'm not saying your vendor is cheating you, but I'm saying with as much as you buy, you should be able to purchase them at bulk pricing, or maybe there's an opportunity to build them on-site."

"From scratch?" said Ghost.

"Yes, I've done some research, and a lot of bike builders are starting to do that. I don't mean the mechanical pieces necessarily, but the forks, tanks, frames, seats, all of that could be done by someone familiar with ironworks."

"Damn, Tinley," said Tango with a grin, "that's impressive, honey. So, does this mean we charge less for the bikes?"

"No! Absolutely not. Your bikes and cars have a reputation, and people are willing to pay the price. What this means is that you will now be making a larger profit. On the last bike you did, the profit was roughly eleven thousand, including man hours, parts, etc. With what we think we can save in prices through the vendor, it would be around eighteen thousand, and if we built some of these items on-site, it could be double that."

"Ho-lee-shit." Skull looked at the spreadsheets and pointed to one of the lines mumbling to the men sitting next to him. "The paints, what the fuck? Why didn't I notice this? He's charging me for custom mixes, but I'm the one who mixes the paints, not him!"

"Don't beat yourselves up. You're not trained to look for this stuff. I am. I think we can triple the profit of all of the businesses by switching vendors or doing some of this in-house. George and Mary will be starting an herb and vegetable garden in the spring. That will cut down on the costs of fresh produce. We're switching our liquor and beer vendors as well. If you guys looked a little further into this, I think we can really find some great savings.

"Also, if you all agree in the next meeting, we will make the part of the organization who helps kidnapping victims, trafficked women and children, that sort of thing, we will make that part of the organization into a non-profit with the name Steel Freedom."

"Jesus, Tinley, this is really the shit. I mean, no telling how much money we've lost in the last seven years because we weren't looking close enough," said Skull.

"That's why you need a professional," she smiled. "It's what I do, and I love what I do."

"Would you consider doing it full-time for us, Tinley?" asked Ghost. Smiling, she looked at the men around the table and nodded.

"I think my fiancée would be very happy if I did that," she grinned.

"Alright then, let's take a look at all of our parts and start thinking about whether or not we can do this shit on-site and what we would need to invest to make it happen. If not, what are some other vendors we can use? If we need to negotiate with current vendors, let Tinley and Kat loose on them."

Tinley gathered the stacks of folders and spreadsheets, her laptop tucked under her arm.

"Tinley?" said Ghost. Looking up at him, she grinned. "Fucking awesome job."

CHAPTER THIRTY-TWO

The pain was excruciating. Everything on her body hurt. She'd taken some of the drugs they offered. She was never opposed to getting a little high. Whatever it was, it had made her feel more adventurous than usual, and she definitely tolerated more pain than usual. That is until she started coming out of it. The problem was that the men were taking so much of the shit, she was amazed they were even still standing, let alone getting hard.

Valerie was used to fucking two or three men at a time, but she'd never had four men abuse her body in so many different ways. She'd certainly let each one fuck her in a different hole, but the fourth man was basically beating her as the other three raped her. It was no longer consensual. They were now officially raping and brutalizing her body. Tied to the kitchen table, naked, bleeding, and cold, she prayed that someone would find her, that maybe one of her roommates would realize she was missing, but the longer the night went on, the less hope remained.

"Wh-what do you want?" she cried.

"Told you. Want to know where this whore is," said Dawg. Tinley looked at the photo again, knowing who it was. Two days ago, she would have gladly given the names of the women in those photos and where they were. Now, knowing what these men were capable of, she was less willing to do so. There was no love lost between her and Keegan, but she also wasn't going to turn her over to these men.

"I-I don't know. I told you it was a New Year's Eve party. There were a lot of people there. This was just a random photo."

"Who are the men with them?"

"Just some guys that w-work at the bar," she lied. He nodded, frowning at the girl. Turning, he turned on the front burner of the stove, letting the gas flames lick the cool cabin air. Pulling out his knife, he let the blade touch the blue and yellow flame, turning it carefully, watching the metal heat up.

Valerie couldn't see what he was doing, but she heard the sound of the stove, and panic bubbled up inside her.

"P-please... let me go... I won't tell anyone. I g-gave you a good time, right? We had fun."

"Yea, you were good, bitch," sneered Cash, twisting one of her nipples so hard she cried out. "You don't get it yet, do you? I like it when you scream. It makes me hard." He unzipped his jeans again and shoved his long cock into her anus. She was already bleeding from her previous encounter with Toad, but he didn't give a shit. She liked the pain, and he was going to give it to her.

"Keep bangin' her," grinned Dawg. "I'm gonna make some pretty pictures on her." He lay the heated knife against her skin, and she screamed in agony. The smell of burning flesh filled her nostrils. He lifted the blade, skin sticking to metal, and heated it once more, burning the flesh off of it. She was barely conscious as he lay the blade against her skin again.

"P-please," she begged, barely able to breathe. Dawg gripped her hair, tilting her head back as Cash just continued to slam into her.

"Tell. Me. Where," he said through a clenched jaw, spittle flying at her face.

"Club Steel..."

"We know that, bitch. Club Steel is where the party was," said Toad.

"N-no, they have homes there. That's where they live," she gasped, crying. Unable to remain alert any longer, she passed out from the pain. Dawg nodded.

"So, they live on the land of the club? Interesting, sounds like we got ourselves some wannabe bikers, brothers. What do you say we show them what a real club looks like?"

"Fuck yea," said Coop. "What do we do about her?" Dawg let his knife trace her skin, the tip outlining the burns on her body and then up toward her breasts.

"You know, I was never a fan of fake tits," he sneered at her body. "Or fake hair." The others grinned and took out their own knives.

Mercifully, Valerie never regained consciousness. Her butchered body tossed behind the bar where she worked, the men returned to the cabin to wipe up the mess, shower, and get some sleep before they paid someone an intimate visit.

CHAPTER THIRTY-THREE

Three weeks. It had been three weeks of hot sex every night and on most days. Tinley and Ty couldn't seem to not touch one another, and if the smile on her daughter's face was any indication, neither could Keegan and Ryan.

While he went to the shop to work, she soaked in the big tub, her body screaming for some relief. She'd made an appointment to see Gabi in an hour, almost positive that she had a bladder infection from all the sex.

Smiling, she touched her sensitive nipples and sucked in a breath. Ty enjoyed them, that's for sure. She let her hand slide over the full mounds, surprised at how tender her body had become. Sitting up in the tub, she swallowed.

"Oh shit," she whispered. Stepping out of the warm water, she dried herself off and dressed. Pulling on her winter coat, she walked out to the long walkway and toward the clinic, entering from the property side.

"Hi, Tinley," said Gabi. "Take a seat, honey. I'm just finishing up with this chart." Tinley nodded, taking the seat Gabi indicated, and then turning, handed her a cup.

"You said you thought you had a bladder infection? Let's get a sample."

"Yea, um, could you run a pregnancy test as well?" she asked.

"Already!" she laughed. "You go, girl. That's awesome, Tinley. Yes, I'll run a test." Tinley left the sample next to the microscope and then went into the exam room, removing her clothes for Gabi. A few minutes later, Gabi entered.

"You definitely have a urinary tract infection. My guess is not having sex for fifteen years and then having it non-stop for three weeks will do that to a girl," she giggled. "I'm going to write you a prescription and suggest that you drink a lot of water, and I find that cranberry juice helps a lot."

"And?" Gabi smiled.

"Congratulations."

"Oh God," she whispered. "I mean, I knew. I-I suspected. I mean, we haven't used protection so..."

"Tinley? You're happy about this, aren't you, honey?"

"Y-yes... it's just..."

"Your age?" She nodded, biting her lower lip. "Tinley, millions of women are having babies at your age, and the births are healthy, normal children. We'll take all the precautions with your pregnancy. We won't do a sonogram or ultrasound until you're closer to eight to ten weeks, but I'll make sure that everything we need, we have at our fingertips and is used." Nodding again, she looked up at Gabi.

"I'm having a baby... at forty."

"Grace is almost forty-three, sweetie. This will be her third pregnancy. Bree is almost thirty-seven. I was thirty-eight when the twins were born."

"I-I guess I didn't realize that," she whispered. "What will people say, Gabi? Ty is such a... a..."

"Hot stud? God? Melt-in-your-mouth dream machine?" Tinley laughed.

"Wow, you've been thinking way too much about my fiancée. Yes, he's all those things and more. He's so damn handsome, and his body, good lord, that body makes me blush every time I see it. But he's also smart and sweet and considerate. He's the most generous lover I've ever known. Although, that's not fair since there was only one other."

"Tinley? What is it you see when you look in the mirror?" asked Gabi.

Tinley looked into the other woman's stunningly unique eyes, their translucent blue sparkling in the light of the room. Gabi was the sort of woman that should be gracing covers of beauty magazines. Her unusual features set against her startling hair color and that bodacious curvy body were extraordinary.

"I-I don't know. I see a mom first and foremost."

"Well, that's part of your problem. Honey, you are a mom, but you're a woman first."

"I see brown hair and blue eyes. I have decent lips, I guess. My belly is a little poochy. My hips are too full..."

"Stop, stop right there. Damn, I hate when we women do this to ourselves," said Gabi. "Tinley, you know what I see? I see a woman with a beautiful head of rich, mahogany-colored hair cut in this amazing style that flatters your face. Your eyes are like the Caribbean Sea, this beautiful mix of blue and green swirling. You have these wonderfully natural full breasts, which your fiancée is going to really love in about three months. Your curves are so youthful and yet soft, inviting for any man who looks at you."

"Wow, are you sure you're straight, Gabi?" smirked Tinley. The other woman laughed and nodded.

"Believe me, with my big chocolate sex stick at home, I want nothing to do with anything else. Yes, I'm definitely straight, but I also recognize the beauty in other women, and you're stunning, Tinley. Ty fell in love with you because you were beautiful on the outside. Then he completely fell when he discovered the beauty you are on the inside." Tears softly fell down Tinley's cheeks, and she nodded, gripping Gabi in a big hug.

"Brick screwed with my head bad. Taking my virginity, leaving me not remembering any of that, was the first thing. Then every time after, the way he just used my body, like it was some sort of tool. I'm eternally grateful that he usually used a condom, considering how much action he was getting with the club whores, but still, would see him coming and try to hide. The only reason I didn't fight more was because of Keegan. I just wanted to keep her safe."

"I know, honey, and she knows that too. It's why she's so supportive of you and Ty. She knows that you deserve this love, Tinley. Stop. Questioning. This."

"Okay."

"Okay?" smiled Gabi.

"Okay," she grinned. "I'm having a baby, Ty's baby. I need to tell him tonight." Gabi nodded.

"Why don't you get dressed first, and then we'll talk some more about vitamins and such." Tinley nodded, dressing once again and meeting Gabi in her office. Twenty minutes later, with the vitamins inside her pockets, she exited the door waving at the other woman.

Walking back toward the barn, she smiled, watching her feet kick at the snow, remembering Ty kicking the snow at her that first night. Head down, she slammed into a body in front of her, falling back against the snow. Looking up, she felt the bubble of panic and started crab walking backwards.

"Where you goin', bitch? We got business."

CHAPTER THIRTY-FOUR

Razor, Tango, Gunner, and Skull were working on several projects at once in the garage. They rarely had anyone manning the front desk, simply because they didn't have the manpower. When they heard the bell, they all looked at one another, basically saying in their heads, eenie, meenie, miney, moe.

"Fine, assholes," said Skull. "I'll go." Opening the door leading from the bays into the office, Skull looked up to see four faces he hadn't seen before but was pretty damn certain he knew exactly who they were.

"Afternoon, fellas, what can we do for you?" asked Skull in a cheery voice. Beneath the counter, he hit the speaker button and smiled.

"Lookin' for a girl. She's... she's my sister, and we need to find her," said Dawg.

"Okay, sure. She in trouble or something? Sick?" said Skull, taking a serious tone.

"Naw, just-just haven't seen her in a while and need to get in touch with her. Someone said she might be stayin' here."

"Huh, that right? Well, I can tell you some of us boys live on-site, and a few have wives. Let me see this girl?" Dawg held up his phone, and sure enough, it was the picture of Keegan, Ty, Ryan, and Tinley the night of the party.

"The one with the short hair," he said.

"She doesn't look familiar. Maybe she's in the restaurant."

"The restaurant?" he asked.

"Yea, Club Steel, where that picture was taken. It's a restaurant on the hill behind us. You're welcome to go out the back and along the walkway. Great food, good booze, you'll enjoy yourself." Dawg nodded at him, looking through the glass windows into the shop.

"You build custom bikes?" he asked, suddenly intrigued.

"Sure do," said Skull enthusiastically. If he could keep this guy talking a bit more, everyone would be in place. "Started about five or six years ago and built a name for ourselves. I do most of the painting and chrome work. The other guys are the geniuses behind the motors. We do some custom cars too, but mostly the bikes. No fucking sissy bikes, choppers or hogs only."

"Know that's fuckin' right," growled Dawg. "So, you're sure you haven't seen the girl?"

"Man, we get a lot of women in here. Know what I mean?" grinned Skull. "Chicks like the bikes, and not to brag, but they like my big package." Inside his stomach was churning. He never spoke with such disrespect for women or for himself and his brothers. He knew it was necessary, but still, it didn't sit well with him.

"Yea, man, know what ya mean," said Dawg. "We're gonna have a look around if that's okay. Walk over to the restaurant."

"Yea, man," he said, waving a big arm toward the back doors. "Be my guest."

Skull opened the door leading into the massive work bays. Gunner, Tango, and Razor looked up only briefly, nodding and then putting their heads back down. Dawg and his men were curious about the bikes being built but also had a very set agenda on their minds.

"Right out that way and to the right, boys," said Sku l. Dawg nodded at him, smirking.

"Stupid motherfuckers," murmured Coop. As they moved along the walkway toward the big red barn, Toad nudged him. Turning quietly, they walked in the opposite direction until their target's head slammed into his chest.

"Where you goin', bitch? We got business."

CHAPTER THIRTY-FIVE

"Zulu?"

"What's wrong, baby?"

"Zulu, Tinley just left here, and a man is standing over her on the walkway."

"Know it, baby, lock the clinic down and don't move." He hung up from his wife and turned to see the faces of Eagle and Hawk. "Don't fucking panic. We've got this. Do what you do. Get up on that fucking roof and take out the other three."

Eagle wanted to argue, but he knew Zulu was right. Racing up the stairs to the living quarters, he pulled the chain for the third-floor space and then ran toward the window facing the clinic. Bringing his weapon to his shoulder, he let out a long slow breath.

"Thought you could get away, didn't you, bitch?" he said, stepping toward her as she continued to scoot back.

"I-I wasn't running from you. I was running from Brick," she whispered.

"Brick is dead." Tinley knew all too well that Brick was dead, but she said nothing. "You outed me, you cunt." She shook her head, her hair flying across her face.

"N-no, no, I didn't. I've been gone fifteen years, Dawg. Think about that. I had no reason to out you ten years after I was safe. That would be stupid. It would only lead you to me!"

Dawg wanted to argue, wanted to disagree, but he couldn't. It was gnawing at him this entire time. Why would she tell everyone about him cheating the club after she was long since safe?

"Don't give a fuck. You gotta die, bitch. Get up," he said. Tinley shook her head, backing up on her bottom again. "I said... get... the fuck..."

"Problem out here?" said Zulu, walking toward the four men. They all turned to see perhaps the largest man they'd ever seen. The big beefy dufus in the shop had been a bear of a man, but this guy was something else.

"No problem," smiled Dawg, "my sister fell, and we were just helping her up. Weren't we, honey?" Zulu gave just a hint of a wink at Tinley, and she nodded.

"Y-yes, yes, I fell," she said, stunned.

"See?" he said, reaching down and gripping her upper arm with force, pulling her to her feet. "We'll just be goin' now."

"No need for that," smiled Zulu.

"No offense, friend, but we're leavin'. Four against one." Zulu let a big smile spread across his face, and he laughed. "What's so funny, boy?" That took the grin off his face, and

Zulu stepped forward. Seeing the other three men reach for weapons at their waists, he stopped.

"First of all, don't ever call me 'boy' again. Second, you need to learn to count, 'boy,' because by my count, it's four against fourteen, fifteen if you count my wife, who has a gun pointed at you from that window over there." Dawg eyed the man up and down and then looked behind him, seeing several men standing silently, weapons at the ready.

"Who the fuck are you?" he asked.

"We're the Steel Patriots, former Special Forces, currently pissed-off badass motherfuckers. You touched her. You tried to hurt her. You sold children, abused them. We don't like that shit," said Zulu, sneering at the other men.

Toad's twitchy fingers couldn't stand it any longer, and he reached for his weapon. *THWAP! THWAP!* Two bullets from the sniper rifle hit him in the head, his blood splattering all over the pristine white snow.

Tinley looked at the dead body and knew. She knew that Ty was somewhere watching over her. Pulling on Dawg's hand, she jerked her arm free and stepped back.

"I'm gonna fucking kill all of you," he spat.

"Hard to do when you're dead," said Ghost, walking up. "Let me introduce myself. I'm Eric Stanton, retired Navy SEAL, and this is my team. Everyone calls me Ghost."

The eyebrows of Cash and Coop rose. They'd heard of this man and knew of his reputation, which did not bode well for them.

"Don't fuckin' care. Bitch is mine," growled Dawg. Ghost shook his head again, turning to the other two men.

"You got one shot. Get your shit and leave here. Ride until your ass hurts, and then keep riding. If I ever see your faces again, I'll kill you." Coop looked at Cash and then back at the other man.

"Born brothers, die as brothers, man," he said, reaching for his weapon. *THWAP! THWAP!* Two more bullets from another direction, and he was down. Cash cursed under his breath and shrugged his shoulders.

"Blaze of glory," he whispered, attempting to pull his weapon. It never even left the holster. He was lying dead before he even touched it.

"Now," said Ghost, "I appreciate brotherhood as much as the next man. That was just foolhardy. I gave them the chance to leave. You don't get that shot." Dawg reached back for Tinley, only to find the big goofy asshole from the shop standing in front of her, blocking his path.

"Don't mistake me for being a nice man," said Skull. "I will fucking break you."

"So what? You're gonna just shoot me here?" said Dawg. No one said anything, not a word. Staring at the man, he displayed his true cowardice, trying to back away and run. Except there was nowhere to run to. Every direction, there was a man bigger than the next. No matter where he looked, his exit was blocked.

He never saw it, never felt it, but three bullets passed silently through his chest as he wheezed, falling on the snow next to his brothers. Hawk walked up and knelt down, the man gasping for air as blood oozed from his mouth.

"How did you find her?" he asked.

"B-bitch... Val... Valerie... whore p-paid..." That was the last sound Dawg made. Life slipped from his body, and Tinley raced down the walkway, throwing herself in Eagle's arms.

"Are you okay, baby? Did he hurt you?" he said, kissing her face.

"N-no, we need to get back to Gabi..."

"Gabi? Why?"

"I-I'm pregnant. I fell..." Before she could say another word, he lifted her, carrying her into the clinic. The others watched them, smiling, and then looking back at the carnage, frowned. Looking up at Ghost, they waited.

"Bury them."

CHAPTER THIRTY-SIX

"Everything is fine, Tinley," said Gabi, tapping her knees to get her to push back on the table. Ty stood at her head, helping her to sit up. He cradled her against his big body. "The fall was a simple fall, and you did the right thing by protecting your body."

"Do we know if it's twins yet?" asked Ty excitedly. Gabi chuckled.

"No, sweetie, we don't. We won't know for a while yet, but keep in mind, Ty, that even though you're a twin, it doesn't mean you'll necessarily have twins."

"I'm having twins," he said definitively.

"Okay, okay," she said, lifting her hands in defeat. "You can get dressed. You're fine to go home. Take it easy, but do your normal activities. Don't deprive yourself of food you might want, but don't overdo activity." She smiled at the couple and left them alone to get dressed.

Tinley started to pull on her clothes, but Ty grabbed her, holding her naked body against his.

"You scared the fuck out of me," he whispered. Tinley looked up to see tears in his eyes.

"I'm okay," she murmured. He nodded, trailing kisses in her hair, along her jaw, and then on her lips. "I'm okay, Ty. Really, I am. We're having a baby, honey."

He let out a loud whoop and yell and then laughed.

"Yes! We're having a baby. My baby is having a baby," he smiled. He released her, allowing her to pull her clothes on once again. Walking back toward the barn, he held her firmly against his body, terrified that she might fall again. The bodies were already gone. The bloodstained snow had somehow disappeared.

Entering the barn, the entire team was seated, looking up at them, waiting to hear that all was okay.

"We're fine," said Tinley.

"We're pregnant!" yelled Ty. She laughed, shaking her head. He turned her in his arms, whispering in her ear. "We're pregnant."

Congrats were heard around the room as everyone gathered once again for a meal and discussion. Ghost explained that the four men were dealt with. The threats against Tinley and Keegan were gone. There should be no further issues. Just as he said it, Sheriff Webb came through the door.

"Sheriff," said Ghost. "What do we owe the pleasure?"

"Folks, nice to see you all." He looked around the room and squinted at Ty and Ryan. "Which one of you is Ryan?"

"I am," he said, stepping forward.

"You had issues with Valerie Todal?" Ryan frowned. It was the first time he'd ever heard her last name. Once more, he was disgusted with his previous self but happy that he'd changed in time to find Keegan.

"Yea, a few of us had some issues. Kat filed a restraining order against her," he said. The sheriff nodded.

"Yep. Knew that. Just letting you folks know she was found brutally murdered. Her body was dumped behind the bar where she worked in the valley."

Murmurs of surprise filtered through the group. Dawg said something about Valerie telling him where they were, but he obviously beat that out of her and then killed her. As hard as he tried to hate her, Ryan felt some sense of sadness for the young woman. If her last few hours were with Dawg and his men, then they were not pleasant hours at all.

"She didn't have any siblings. Her roommates are taking care of her burial. Thought you should know, though, in her bedroom closet, she had hundreds of photos of the two of you," he said, pointing to Hawk and Eagle. "There were a couple of the women, you and you." He pointed to Tinley and Keegan.

"Holy shit," grumbled Eagle.

"She had other photos, so don't feel special. Pictures of you," he said, pointing to Skull, "and you." He pointed to Axe.

"Christ, she really was unhinged," said Hawk.

"Appears that way. Anyway, her roommates didn't even know. I can tell you no matter what she did to all of you, that poor girl didn't deserve what was done to her body."

"Thank you for telling us, Sheriff." Ghost was basically dismissing the man. They didn't need to know the details. Tinley and Keegan, of all the people, didn't. He nodded, turning to leave.

When the room was filled with just the Steel Patriots once again, they returned to their meal and to the company of one another. Ghost felt the familiar burning in his gut. The feeling that happened when he was forced to take a life. He didn't have a problem with it, especially with someone threatening his family, but he damn sure thought when he left the service, it might be the end of it.

George walked into the dining room and smiled.

"Dinner will be ready in a minute. For now, y'all need to come see somethin'." They all stood, following George toward the daycare room where Mary kept the children most days. Quietly opening the door, they all looked at the bodies lying out on the mat.

Calla was in the middle, one arm around JT, the other around Wade. Tyler's body curled over her head, their little hands all touching. Black, white, pink. It didn't matter. The men all looked at one another, the women smiling.

"That's what it's all about," said George softly, "that right there, unequivocal love."

CHAPTER THIRTY-SEVEN

Keegan was so happy to be curled in Ryan's arms in the cottage. She curled her feet beneath her, her head laying against his chest as they watched a movie. She loved this place. The space was perfect for the two of them, and the style was exactly what she would choose for herself.

"I guess I can go back to work tomorrow," she said softly. He nodded, frowning.

"Yea. I guess."

"I have to work, Ryan," she said, lifting her head. "I like my work."

"I know. I mean, I know you like your work, but..."

"But?"

"What if we built a shop for you here? Then you could be right here on the property all the time. I wouldn't worry about you as much, and when we decide to have kids, you'll be close." She smiled, nodding. She sensed that he might ask for something like this.

"I can see that as an advantage. It's not that much further for my clients to come, and I might attract new business from the communities up the mountain." Ryan smiled, feeling the weight lessen on his chest. "What about where I live? I mean, Mom and I share that house right now, but I know that her and Ty will be building here or something. If I work here, I don't want to live in town."

"You wouldn't," he said firmly. "I asked Ghost if I could buy the cottage."

"Y-you did?"

"Yep. I like our little cottage. The heat in that other room needs to be fixed, but we'll make sure we get that done before any babies come. It needs a good coat of paint, and maybe the floors need to be redone, but it's a great little place. Don't you think?" he asked expectantly.

"I-I do, but what if we have more than one baby. There's only one spare room."

"No problem. We'll add on as many rooms as we need. We'll have plenty of land to spread out. I want this, baby. I want this with you."

"Yea," she said, nodding as she wiped a tear. "Yea, I want that too. Ryan, I can't believe this. Three weeks ago, I thought you were an egotistical, narcissistic asshole, and now, I can't imagine my life without this caring, loving, sexy man seated beside me."

"I still got an ego, baby," he grinned. "Like I know you love my big dick." Keegan laughed, nodding.

"You got me there. I do love that big dick."

"Good. That's settled. We're getting married in a few days. When are you going to stop your birth control?" he asked.

"Ryan! I'm twenty-two, honey. How about we wait a year or so. Let's get settled as a married couple. Enjoy each other for a while first. Besides, Mom and Ty are pregnant right now. With them, Kat and Whiskey, Bree and Doc, Ghost and Grace, and Taylor and Tango pregnant, that's a lot of new babies coming into the compound at once." He nodded, kissing his way down her neck, feeling himself stiffen with just the scent of her skin.

"Mmmm, you smell good," he growled.

"Ryan, did... did you hear me..." she asked breathlessly.

"Yep, heard you. Doesn't mean I agree. Take your clothes off."

"Ryan, everything can't be solved by getting naked Just because you order me to get naked doesn't mean you get what you want. I, oh, shit, yes, touch that again..."

"What were you saying?" he grinned against her nipple.

"Fuck, you don't play fair," she said, pulling her shirt over her head. He shoved her sleep pants down, her bare ass now available for him. Pulling her to his lap, straddling his big thighs, he slapped her ass cheek. She startled but smiled, taking his mouth forcefully.

"Thought you said I didn't play fair," he grinned.

"Shut up and fuck me."

CHAPTER THIRTY-EIGHT

Tinley decided not to tell Ty that she had an appointment with Gabi today. It was mid-March, and spring was definitely in full swing.

Their wedding, along with Ryan and Keegan's, took place just as she imagined. Standing on the outlook, the valley covered in snow below them, she walked down the long, carpeted aisle in an ivory one-piece jumpsuit with a faux-fur color. Her hair was laced with baby's breath and white roses. Ty wore dark jeans, crisp white shirt, and blazer with his cowboy boots. Exactly what she'd asked for. When he slid on the diamond wedding band, she gasped at the beautiful rings on her fingers. His band of a solid black titanium seemed to suit him perfectly.

Keegan wore a white column gown with lace insets at the back and neck. Ryan was dressed exactly like his brother. He placed an emerald and diamond ring on her finger with the band to match. Having ordered it custom-made, it was the first time she saw it. She cried so hard, they had to give her a moment to gather herself. George gave Tinley away; Skull gave Keegan away.

"How are you feeling" asked Gabi.

"Great, fat, but great," she smiled. "I'm starving all the time and craving the most outrageous things."

"Like?"

"Liver and onions, peanut butter and apples, and gouda cheese."

"At the same time?" asked Gabi.

"No," she laughed. "Definitely not. I never craved anything with Keegan, so this is all new to me."

"Okay, well, let's see what we have. Are you ready?" smiled Gabi. Tinley nodded as she passed the wand over her belly and smiled bigger. Speaking to Tinley softly, the other woman could only nod. "Don't change anything you're doing, Tinley. Don't deprive yourself, just get more rest maybe. You're going to need it."

Tinley walked along the path toward the shop, stepping into the bay to see Ty speaking with Skull. He smiled, taking in the cute little belly already protruding from her body.

"Hey, baby, you feeling okay?" he said, kissing her.

"Yea, I-I have something to tell you," she said. "I just had a visit with Gabi."

"Fuck, I knew it!" he yelled, getting the attention of every man in the garage. "We're having twins, aren't we?" Everyone cheered, and then Tinley shook her head.

"N-no, no, we're not having twins," she said, holding his arm.

"We aren't? I was so sure." He looked so disappointed. She wanted to cry for him. "Is everything okay? Are you and the baby okay?"

"Uh, yea, babies."

"Babies? But you said..."

"Triplets, we're having triplets..." she said, smiling at him.

"Trip... three... three babies," he uttered softly.

"YES!" screamed Ryan. "I'm going to be an uncle to three at one time! Fucking awesome!" Tinley smiled at her brother-in-law/son-in-law, although they tried not to label what they were to one another.

"Ty? Honey, say something. Tyran O'Neal, I need for you to be okay with this because I can damn sure tell you this is the last time I'm getting pregnant. Ty? My body cannot take more than this. Three babies, Ty. How am I going…" Her breath was taken as his mouth slammed against her own. He nibbled on her lips as he lifted her off her feet, cradling her body against his.

"We're having triplets," he said, kissing her again, tears rolling down his cheeks.

"Y-yes, are you okay with this?" she said, kissing away his tears.

"I'm fucking thrilled. We're going to be so happy, baby. I bought the cabin from Ghost," he said, smiling.

"You did?" Her shocked face told him that he'd done the right thing. For weeks now, he and the guys had been working on renovating the place, insulating the walls, expanding the cabin, securing the deck, and modernizing the kitchen and bathroom. With the help of Grant and his construction crew, the one-bedroom log cabin was now a three-bedroom gorgeous modern home.

"I did, baby. You said you fell in love with it during our honeymoon, so I made an offer to Ghost, and he accepted. The guys and I, and Grant, we've been working on it for weeks now. We can move in whenever you're ready, Tinley."

"Oh my God," she said, feeling the tears rush to her eyes. "Oh, damn hormones." He still had not put her down, and she tapped him on the shoulder.

"Nope, not putting you down, honey. Not until we get to our bed. We can still make love, right?" Tinley laughed at that, tossing her head back.

"Yes, we definitely can." Leaning into his ear, she whispered. "Pregnancy hormones make you horny as a cat in heat. I'm pregnant times three. I want to fuck!"

"Boys, I'm outta here," he hollered as they left the rcom. "So, we can always build more bedrooms later."

"Ty? Three babies, honey, three. No more." He grirned, kissing her as he walked with her in his arms.

"We'll talk about it later."

CHAPTER THIRTY-NINE

In the span of just three weeks, four new lives screamed their little lungs out at the compound. First was a healthy baby girl born to Doc and Bree. Eva Irene was eight pounds and one ounce. Her flaming red curls gave no doubt as to who her mother was.

Forty-eight hours later, Whiskey and Kat gave birth to another girl, Juliette Rose, seven pounds even. Her white-blonde hair so much like her mother's, her hazel eyes like her father's.

Four days later, Taylor and Tango gave birth to a boy, Chase Maxwell. Six pounds, six ounces of pure little boy.

And finally, just one week later, Ghost and Grace gave birth to a second son, Eric Ryan. Grace insisted on having her tubes tied while she was there, and Gabi gladly obliged. Eight children, seven under the age of eighteen months, now graced their compound. Three more were on the way in the summer.

Tinley walked every day, ensuring that she got her exercise in. She was doing extremely well with her weight and blood pressure, everyone very happy with how she was handling the pregnancy. While reviewing some of the invoices at the shop, she sat at the front desk, her feet propped up on a stool.

Ty would pop in every thirty minutes or so, rub her belly and talk to the babies, give his wife a kiss, and then go back to work. George brought lunch over for her, making sure she didn't move around too much. As the bell above the door rang, she stood to see a tiny little woman enter.

"Hello, welcome to Steel. Can I help you?" she said in a perky little voice.

"I hope so," she said, smiling at the other woman. Tinley couldn't help but think she looked like Tinkerbell. She couldn't be more than five-feet-two, her tight body reminding her of a gymnast. She had blonde hair curling down her back and the biggest green eyes she'd ever seen. "I'm looking for someone named Skull."

"Oh, yes, Skull. Scott is his real name. Let me get him for you." She opened the door to the garage and called for Skull, who looked up and smiled at Tinley, walking toward her.

"What's up? You need anything?" he asked.

"No, there's a woman here to see you."

"A woman? For me?" he said incredulously.

"Yes," she laughed, "is that so unusual?"

"Well, yea, but I'll come in. Give me a minute to wipe my hands." Tinley nodded and walked back into the office.

"He'll be right with you. I'm Tinley, by the way. My husband works here as well."

"Willa," she said, smiling. "How much longer for you?"

"Oh, well, longer than you think. I'm having triplets."

"Oh my God!" she gasped. "Really?"

"Really, my husband is a twin. He and his brother both live here, and, well, it sounds strange, but my daughter from a first relationship is married to his brother."

"Wow, interesting at Christmas, right?"

"No doubt," laughed Tinley. "Oh, here he is. Scott? This is Willa. Willa... Scott."

You could have knocked all two hundred and fifty pounds of him over with a feather. Skull stared at the little pixie, his heart beating so hard against his chest, he was certain she could hear it. Her smile was so wide and bright, he could feel himself hardening in his coveralls.

"Scott?" yelled Tinley.

"Oh, sorry," he said, reaching out a hand. Her tiny hand was lost inside his. "Scott Crawford, but they call me Skull. We've been communicating back and forth on e-mail and text."

"Yes, sorry about not calling ahead of time. I just moved here a few weeks ago to be closer to my brothers. I was hoping maybe you could show me the design so far." He nodded, opening the door for her. As she stepped through, all eyes turned to her and then back to Skull, who shook his head slightly.

Pulling back the tarp, he revealed the sleek motorcycle, chrome gleaming in the light of the garage. The tank wasn't finished yet, but the design of the Army logo surrounded by all the medals and ribbons her brother received was exactly what she'd pictured.

"It's beautiful," she said with tears in her eyes. "Your work is beautiful."

"Thank you," he beamed. She continued to cry and then brought her hands to cover her face. Skull wasn't very experienced with women, but one crying this much he was pretty sure wasn't normal.

"Hey, hey, it's okay. If you don't like something, you can change it," he said. She shook her head, and he reached out, his big paw lightly resting on her shoulder. Willa turned into the heat of his body, burying her face in his lower chest, her head barely hitting his rib cage.

"Whoa, hey, sweetheart, it's okay. What's wrong?" he said, holding her still. By this time, the other men, all noticing that she was crying and not out of happiness, stood from the work they were doing and gathered around Skull and the little woman.

"I don't know what to do," she hiccupped. "My b-brothers... they're m-missing... both of them."

"Okay, okay, one is active duty, right?" he asked. She nodded. "The other retired?" She nodded again. "When did you see them last?"

"M-my first night in town. I rented an apartment in town, and they came over to help me unpack. I could tell something was wrong. They were both nervous and kept looking out the window. When I asked them what was wrong, they wouldn't answer me. They left, and I haven't been able to get a hold of them since. My brother's unit commander said he's AWOL."

"Okay, sweet girl, it's okay," said Skull, gently rubbing her back. "Let's get you home, and we'll figure this out." She started crying again, and he nearly cracked in two at the sound. Shaking her head, she looked up at him, those green eyes begging him.

"I-I can't. Someone broke into my apartment last night, trashed everything. I stayed at a bed and breakfast last night. I-I don't know what to do. I have no one. I have nowhere to go."

"Sure, you do, honey," he said resolutely. "You have me."

EXCERPT FROM SKULL

Scott Timothy Crawford could not be further from the vision of someone you would think of as a Coast Guard officer. Usually, those men were lean swimmers. Average build, average height. Not Scott. Scott was built like a professional wrestler. His chest was so wide, they had to custom make his uniforms, his thighs thick as tree trunks.

Where he surprised everyone was in his ability to outswim almost anyone who challenged him. With a love of swimming since the age of four, Scott grew up around the water, spending his life with his hair wet and his fingers and toes wrinkled.

Now standing across from this tiny woman, a woman that no doubt if he rolled over on top of in bed, he'd crack her in half. She was barely to his lower rib cage, her maybe five-feet-two, to his six-foot-five. Her long wavy blonde hair shone like a wheat field at sunrise, her green eyes staring into his own brown ones. The tears being shed by those green eyes are what was killing him right now.

Face down drug traffickers, no problem. Shoot a kidnapper, no problem. Rescue a boat of refugees, piece of cake. Handle a crying woman, shit!

OTHER BOOKS BY MARY KENNEDY YOU MIGHT ENJOY!

REAPER Security Series
Erin's' Hero
Lauren's Warrior
Lena's' Mountain
Sara's' Chance
Mary's Angel
Kari's Gargoyle
Rachelle's Savior
Adele's Heart
Tori's' Secret
Finding Lily
Montana Rules
Savannah Rain
Gray Skies
My First Choice
Three Wishes
Second Chances
One Day at a Time
When You Least Expect It
Missing Hearts
Trail of Love

Steel Patriots MC Series
Ghost – Book One
Doc – Book Two
Whiskey – Book Three
Zulu – Book Four
Gunner – Book Five
Tango – Book Six
Razor – Book Seven
Ace – Book Eight

My SEAL Boys (connections to the REAPER Series)
Ian
Noa
Carter
Lars
Trevor
Fitz
Chris
O'Hara

Strange Gifts Series
Dark Visions
Dark Medicine
Dark Flame

ABOUT THE AUTHOR

Mary Kennedy is the mother of two adult children, has an amazing son-in-law, and is grandmother to two beautiful grandsons. She works full-time at a job she loves, and writing is her creative outlet. She lives in Texas and enjoys traveling, reading, and cooking. Her passion for assisting veterans and veteran causes comes from a strong military family background. Mary loves to hear from her readers and encourages them to join her mailing list, as she'll keep you up-to-date on new releases at https://insatiableink.squarespace.com. You can also join her Facebook page at Insatiable Ink.

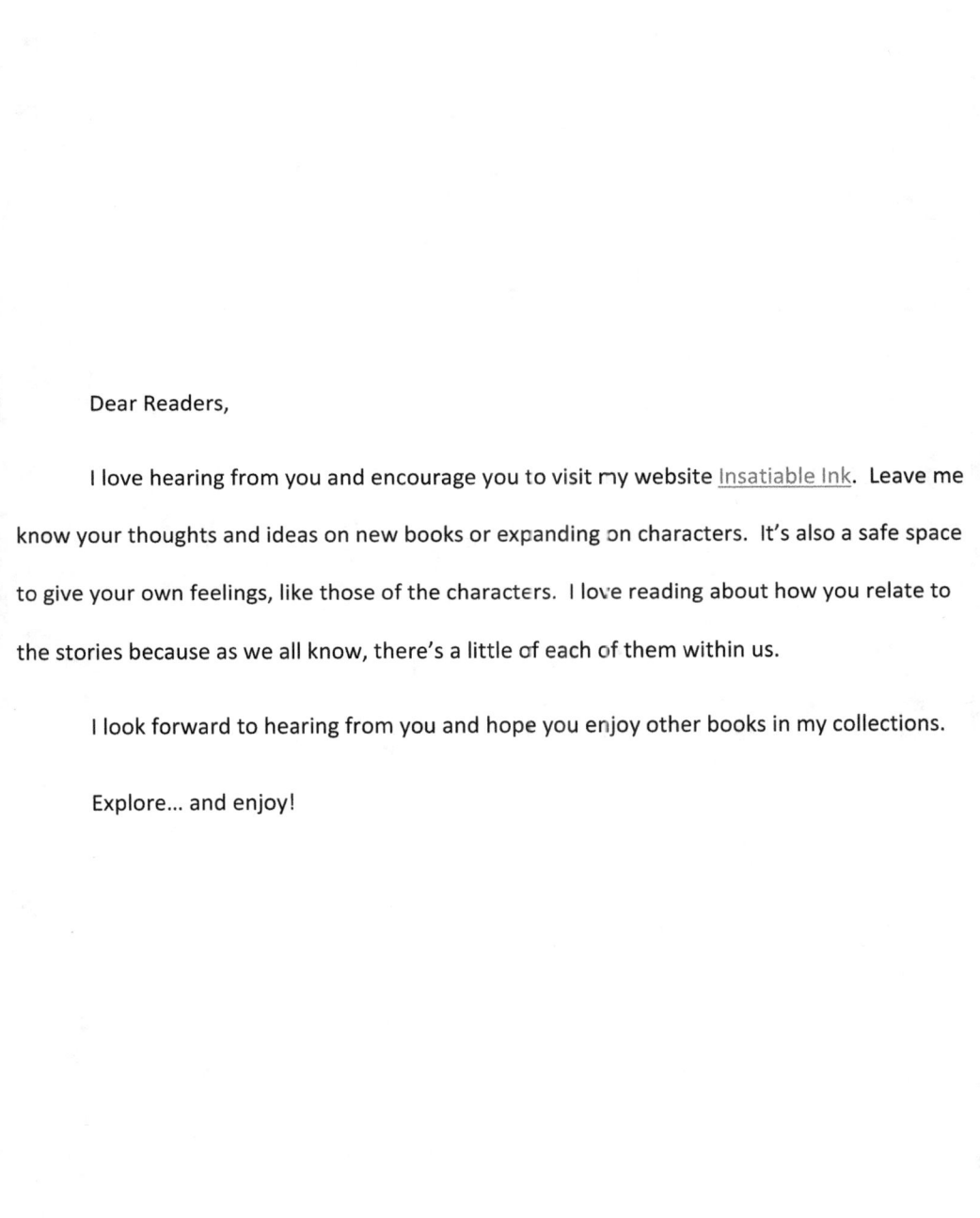

Dear Readers,

I love hearing from you and encourage you to visit my website [Insatiable Ink](). Leave me know your thoughts and ideas on new books or expanding on characters. It's also a safe space to give your own feelings, like those of the characters. I love reading about how you relate to the stories because as we all know, there's a little of each of them within us.

I look forward to hearing from you and hope you enjoy other books in my collections.

Explore... and enjoy!

www.ingramcontent.com/pod-product-compliance
Lightning Source LLC
Chambersburg PA
CBHW071506170626
46811CB00007B/2748